Summer Vibes In Brooklyn

Short Story By: Kellz Kimberly

Social Media

Facebook: Kellz Kimberly
Facebook Reading Group: I Read, I Sip, I
Slay
Instagam: Kellzkimberlyxoxo
Twitter: xoKellzKxo

Keisha Harper

"**I** got a bitch name Keisha, she a real dick pleasure," I heard the second I walked into the spot.

The niggas in the weed spot loved to play games like I wasn't the type of chick to slap a nigga for disrespecting me. Out of everyone in here, Eddy was the worse. He stayed trying to get at me but never came at me with the respect I deserved. He figured because he had money, I was supposed to fall to my knees and suck his dick on command. Now, I know a few chicks who got down like that, but I'd never been that pressed. I didn't care how much I was in need, this nigga would never get the privilege of saying he had my body. I was too damn elite for the lames.

"Wassup Keisha, you not gon' speak? How you gon' do a nigga greasy after I sang ya theme song?" he laughed, along with another dude who was in the room.

Trying to keep my attitude in check because this was business, I smacked my lips and replied, "Stop playing with me, Eddy. Whatever Keisha you're speaking on ain't *this* Keisha. The wonders these lips work, you'll never experience."

"She could be you if you stop playing. The confidence is golden, but a nigga don't need allat."

"I'm sure you don't," I giggled.

"You gon' stop playing or what?"

1

"Playing is the last thing I do and you should know that. When I say I don't want you, it's because I really don't want you. Stop confusing the push away with the chase."

"Yeah ight, that's what all you hoes say. Then, once I throw a lil bank ya way, the tune starts to sound real different. Ain't that right Jeezy?"

Like a dog hearing his name being called, a fine ass chocolate Adonis came walking out of the back. It was a shame that he was a worker because if he had been a shot caller, I probably would've gave him that work. He was tall as fuck and rocked a dark Caesar that connected to a full beard. His beard was cut close but framed his lips perfectly. The dark color of his eyes was hypnotizing but not enough to cause me to look past the fact that he came running when another nigga called him.

"Jeezy, tell Keisha how these hoes be out here giving it up.

"He doesn't have to tell me shit because I'm not one of them hoes."

"Then, what you doing in the spot? Females only come up here when they trying to fuck or suck for some weed," Jeezy said, eyeing me lustfully.

"Fix ya face. I'm here to pick up my shit, so I can make my own money. What a nigga can throw my way never moved me," I corrected.

"So if I give you a stack right now, you wouldn't fuck a nigga?" Eddy questioned.

"No."

"What about ten?"

"Ten what?"

"Ten stacks to suck my dick right now."

"You got it on you?"

"Come on ma, you shouldn't have to ask. To sweeten the pot, I'll throw in a few extra packs and you can keep a hundred percent of the profit."

"Show me the money," I purred, biting the corner of my lip.

"Jeezy, go get that."

Before walking away, this nigga shook his head and hit me with a disapproving stare like I gave a fuck about what he thought. He came back a minute or two later with ten stacks and sat it on the table.

"We have a deal?"

"Yeah, we have a deal."

I licked my lips, then walked over to him and dropped his basketball short and briefs. I pulled his dick out and the only one who had a problem was Jeezy.

"Ayo," he gritted. "You really gonna sit here and watch this shit?"

"It's not like I ain't never seen a bitch suck some dick before," the other dude said. "Fuck I'm leaving for when I'm trying to get mine sucked too?"

"You wildin'. Eddy, hit my line later if you change your mind. You got 24."

Laughing, he replied, "My answer won't change lil nigga."

Jeezy walked out with a frown on his face and I dropped to my knees, ready to earn my money.

"Be easy on a nigga and I might add a little extra green."

"Don't worry. I got you, daddy."

I took his dick in my hand and, to my surprise, it was bigger than I thought but skinny like a pencil. I brought it up to my lips and, before it could touch my skin, the blade I held between my teeth sliced less than an inch off the tip.

"Ahh fuck!" he screamed, then pushed my head away.

The other dude in the room look terrified, causing my laughter to grow. Both these niggas were some birds and the way they talked to women was disgusting. The little that I sliced didn't come close to what his ass deserved, but it was gonna have to do.

"Snatch her ass up and lock her in the back. Then, bring the car around; I gotta get to the hospital."

"Nigga, you good?" Ole boy asked.

"Does it fucking look like I'm good? Do what the fuck I said and don't ask no more stupid questions."

Ole boy looked like he was about to reach out in my direction, so I swung the blade, catching his arm.

"Ah fuck, that bitch sting!" he yelped.

"Nigga, you can't be serious," Eddy huffed, still holding his bleeding dick.

"Fuck you mean? She sliced my muthafucking arm."

While they went back and forth, I picked up five of the stacks and dipped out. Both of them niggas came off as pussy, but I knew better than to push my luck. A snippet of his dick and 5 G's was nothing to Eddy. Word around

Bedstuy was this nigga had big bank and was climbing his way up to be the king of Brooklyn. Whether that was true or not didn't matter because no real nigga was gonna be pressed over 5 grand and, if he was, then fuck it; I would see him when I see him.

"You finish quick," I heard a raspy voice say from behind me.

"Or that nigga was just easy to get off."

"That nigga played you, didn't he?" he questioned, then snatched my Michael Kors bag from me.

"Nigga, what is you doing?"

"How you suck a nigga off and only get half the money he offered you and none of the weed? Whoever taught you the game fucked up," he chuckled.

"I'm sorry, do I know you? I ask because you're paying too much attention to a situation that ain't got shit to do with you. What, you mad it wasn't your dick I was sucking on?" I asked, running my tongue across my lips.

"Baby, if I wanted my dick down your throat, it would be down ya throat," he replied so smoothly.

I swear if this was any other day or a different situation, this nigga could've got the coochie.

"Trust me when I tell you it wouldn't be that easy. But, if you don't mind, I have places to be and muthafuckers to see."

I held my hand out, letting him know he could give me back my bag, but he never caught the hint. Instead of my bag, he tossed a crumbled piece of paper in my hand and started to walk away.

"Nigga, where are you going?" I yelled.

"To make a move. When you're ready, hit my line."

"Hit your line," I mumbled to myself as he disappeared around the block.

Opening the crumbled paper, I saw he left me his number along with a message.

Hit me when you're ready to make some real money.

James 'Jeezy' Brown

After taking the money from ole girl, I headed back to the crib, so I could figure some shit out. A nigga was out here on his last because things weren't hitting the same. Cash was running low and the positions that were being handed my way was disrespectful on all levels. I was too old to be a fucking runner and had way too much respect out here in the city. Muthafuckers must've forgot all the work I had put in and fell asleep on the kid. It was all love though cause I was gonna get back right. Six months or so ago, money wouldn't have been an issue. Shit, six months ago, the money was flowing like fucking water and the flow was never ending.

My boy Casper and I had all of Gravesend on lock. For two years straight, niggas couldn't move without checking in. Everything was on the up and I was ready to take over the whole Coney Island when this nigga told me he was out. He came to me saying he stacked all he needed to change his life and that he was done. Being the arrogant nigga I was, I laughed Casper out the fucking room. I should've took him seriously because when it came time to re-up, he was nowhere to be found and I was short. Worm wasn't trying to co-sign shit and that put me in a fucked up position. Ultimately, I took the L and been trying to get back since.

Casper and I were still tight because when it all boiled down, I couldn't do shit but respect his movements. While I was out here spending money on bullshit, he stacked his and made the right connections to change his life, which was changing his daughter's life at the same time. I couldn't hate on a nigga doing better for his seed, so I took my fuck-up on the chin. That one mistake had changed everything for me. I was hustling backwards like a muthafucker. That shit would never happen again. I was too hungry to put myself in a fucked-up situation for a second time. So, if I had to kick down the door and wave a tech 'round that muthafucker, so be it.

A plan was in place and, by the time summer was over, I would be cakin' once again. Word around C.I. was that Worm gave my spot in Gravesend to some niggas that run with Eddy. I went by his way to talk this out in a civil manner before I used force. Eddy wasn't a threat but, if I could get my spot back without bloodshed, I was gonna try that first. We discussed me taking back my block vaguely before ole girl pulled up. The money I took from her wasn't my come-up but more so hers. She left the spot with half the money she was promised and none of the weed. It wasn't hard to figure out something had went south and she dipped out with half. The money wasn't shit to Eddy, but his pride and ego wasn't gonna allow him to let a chick who did him greasy roam free without consequence. He was gonna come for her and, if she ain't move right, she was gonna get got. The money being in my possession was to ensure a conversation was had between the two of us. The enemy of my enemy was a friend and shawty was looking like public enemy number one.

In the middle of rolling up, a call came through on my phone. I snatched it from the kitchen counter thinking it was shawty and was pissed when I saw it was Casper.

"Fuck you want nigga?" I barked.

"What bitch got ya balls in a knot bruh?" Casper laughed.

"Move with that cause no bitch could ever have me jammed up. Wassup tho?"

"Just checking on you. I know shit been-"

"Don't start with that big brother mess. I told you I was good last week and that still remains."

"I'm just saying if you need me to help you with some moves, just say the word."

"For all that, you should've just stayed a player. I mean, it's not like you all the way out anyway."

"What I do ain't got shit to do with what I'm doing. Looking over my shoulder for shiesty niggas is dead because I'm all the insurance I need to make sure niggas don't jump bad. I'm not a pawn in this muthafucker; I'ma king"

"I feel you," I replied, keeping it short.

I was happy for my bro; I just didn't wanna hear that shit at this moment.

"It could be the same for you if you just-"

"Come on man, you know how I give it up. Being on the outside looking in never been my thing. I like to get my hands dirty, then count my money when it's clean," I laughed.

"Just don't leave them dirty for too long."

"Never," I assured.

Casper and I kicked it on the phone until I heard Cassie in the background demanding this nigga's attention. We hung up with intentions of getting up the next day. Moving from the couch, I was heading for the shower when I got a knock at the door. Not too many people knew where I rested my head, so visitors wasn't something I had often. I eased over to the door with my nine in hand, ready to blast off if need be.

"I'ma need you to get that gun outta my face because we both know your ass ain't shooting shit this pretty," shawty sassed before pushing me to the side and welcoming herself into my home.

"Don't let ya cockiness be the reason you get caught slipping. Pretty or not, a slug is gonna find it's home."

"Yeah, yeah, yeah. Enough of the big boy talk. Where is my money?"

"I got a question of my own first. How'd you find out where I stay?"

Waving her hands around, she giggled and said, "I know you didn't think this place was gonna be hard to find. I understand wanting to be in the cut but, umm, you could've done better than this."

She glanced around my place with nothing but disdain on her face. My shit wasn't A1, but it wasn't no projects either. I had a loft out in Brighten that was paid up and I owned; the bitch was just empty.

"Fix ya face cause this all me. It might not be much or in an uppity neighborhood, but I own this. That's more than a lot of niggas could say."

"Nigga, I don't give a fuck about the location; I'm disgusted with the lack of decor in here. How you own all of this and the only thing in ya living room is a futon, an old ass looking coffee table and that big ass tv on the wall? Do you know what I could do with all of this? Baby, you're not doing this space any justice."

"Fix it for me then," I smirked.

"Give me the money and I'm not talking about the cash you stole."

"I've never stole a day in my life."

"Then, what do you call snatching my bag and walking off with *my* belongings?"

"An investment."

"Funny. Too bad I'm not in the mood. Can I have my money back please?"

"After we have a conversation."

"Didn't we do that already?"

"You talked, I replied, but it wasn't the conversation I wanted to have."

"Hmmm, seems a little personal and I can't help with that. Now, beat ya big ass feet and get me my money. I'm late for a dinner date."

"What pussy nigga you going on a date with?"

Real shit, I had no right questioning her, but a nigga couldn't help it. Taking her in, I was attracted. She gave me Regina Hall vibes when she was that stripper in *The Best Man*. Her beauty was natural but not close to being subtle. Full lips, chinky brown eyes, and freckles were the facial features that caught and held my attention. Her thin slick frame was bodying bitches and I was sure she knew it. Shawty was some fire and stayed talking slick shit. She was my type and a nigga could see himself getting selfish real quick

"Pussy isn't how I like my dudes."

"But, he ain't me."

"And that means what?"

"He pussy," I laughed.

She broke her scowl to laugh and, when that smile hit, my heart skipped a few beats.

"Why are you cheesing so hard? Put those 32's away," she told me, still laughing.

"Chill on my shit; you just got a beautiful smile."

"Don't try to sweet talk me. Can't no man get over on me by telling me what I already know. You can get my money tho."

"Where we going for dinner?"

"You're not coming."

"If you want ya money, then I'm pulling up. Tell homie it's dinner for three. I'ma shower; have things handled by the time I get out."

"Repeat that again."

"No need to. You heard what I said and my baby wouldn't disappoint daddy."

"Don't know who your baby is but go find the bitch."

"Do as I said, ight?"

"Whatever," she huffed and pulled out her phone.

Leaving her to handle that, I went in my room, threw her bag in the safe I had at the back of my closet, and grabbed my shit to jump in the shower.

Keisha

"What you mean a nigga is coming with you to dinner and don't know who he is?" my cousin, Kylie, questioned.

"What kind of hoe shit you have going on?" her twin sister, Bailey, chimed in.

"Listen, if I could explain it to y'all, I would, but shit is all crazy."

"You're gonna have to explain it because you know Ms. Prissy ain't gonna rock with a dude coming to dinner."

"I forgot Phour was supposed to be coming."

Phour was Kylie and Baily's older sister but didn't hang with us like that. I had nothing but love for my cousin and was at her door whenever she needed me; I just couldn't fuck with how she moved. Growing up, we were all close but, as time passed and we started to realize what we wanted in life, Phour started to drift from us and become a person I didn't recognize. She tamed herself, which wasn't a bad thing, but the looking down part of it all didn't work for me. Yet, I still kicked it with her whenever the chance presented itself.

"How you forget that Mr. Proper allowed her to come hang with the ghetto side?" Bailey laughed.

"Because I'm not tripping off him or what he allows her to do. I gotta tell y'all some shit she's not gonna approve of, so I'ma call her and tell her not to come."

"Do that and, while you're at it, find out the name of the man you don't know because I'ma need something to call him."

"His name is Jeezy."

"Jeezy who used to run Gravesend Jeezy?" Kylie questioned.

"I don't know."

"How don't you know?" Kylie sighed.

"Because her ass spends too much time in the Ville."

"I be in Gravesend. I just don't parlay with them hoes. Well, outside of you two hoes," I joked.

"Ya mammy is a hoe!" they shot back in unison.

"So I've been told," I laughed. "Let me call this girl, so she don't show up."

"Cool. Text us when you get to the restaurant."

"Okay, love y'all."

"We love you, too."

Hanging up, I scrolled to Phour's name and was about to call her but changed my mind. I sent her a text instead because I wasn't in the mood to be chastised.

Me: Dinner is canceled. Something came up so the twins and I decided to switch the night.

Phour didn't give me a second to think of the rest of the lie before she was texting me back.

Phour: What came up? I've been looking forward to this dinner. Especially because it's the only lowkey thing I can get the three of you to do.

Me: I have a date

Phour: What hustler you came up on now?

She wasn't even on the phone and I could hear the distaste in her words. Phour had really changed and did little to hide it.

Me: Why it gotta be all of that? How you know I didn't meet a good wholesome dude like your Oreo?

Phour: He's not an Oreo and you would never date someone of James' caliber. You like that hood, cheat on you then fuck you crazy to say sorry type of nigga.

Me: You know me so well

My text was sarcastic but, knowing Phour, she wasn't going to catch on. Instead of continuing to go back and forth with her, I turned my phone off, got up from the couch and headed into his kitchen. Before coming this way, I ate an edible and the munchies were starting to set in. Opening his fridge, I sighed in frustration because his ass ain't have shit. I didn't know what my cousins were talking about because this nigga couldn't have been running a damn thing. His loft seemed pricy and the fact he owned it was admirable, but the lack of things in it had me thinking he was a whole bum. From what I could see, he didn't have not one piece of expensive nothing in this bitch. If I had to guess, he was trying to find a come-up or working on his way up because this wasn't impressive.

"Broke niggas never got food," I mumbled, still looking for something to snack on.

"Why you going through my shit and talking slick?"

I jumped at the sound of his voice because I never heard his footsteps. "What, did you moonwalk in here? Where your footsteps at?"

"Do you ever chill with the snappy replies?"

"Sometimes, but a nigga gotta earn it and, right now, you're not close."

"Good thing I ain't trying to be. You're ready?"

"Yeah, cause I'm hungry," I told him and headed out of the kitchen. I started going towards the door when I realized he didn't have my bag with him.

"Where's my bag?"

"My bad, hold up."

He dipped to the back of the house and came back with my bag. He tossed it my way and, of course, I opened it looking for my money.

"Uh, it's kind of light, don't you think?"

"Nah, you good."

"Okay. The little game you're playing is cute, but where's my money?"

"You'll get that after we have that conversation."

"Then, let's have it now because I'm not-"

"Chill the fuck out. If you need money to pay for your meal, I got you. If you need a little change for gas, I got you. You don't gotta trip over chump change when in the company of a boss."

Bursting out laughing, I took every word this nigga said as a joke because he couldn't be serious. His stern facial expression never changed, which told me he was taking his own hype seriously.

"Look, I don't mean to be disrespectful but newsflash, nothing about you screams boss or that you have money. Let's keep it a bean, my nigga, what boss holds a bitch's five stacks over a conversation that he wants to have? A real boss ass nigga would've gave me my money and then sent five more stacks my way and some roses. That's the kind of conversation a real boss nigga be trying to have. This kiddy shit you doing ain't even on a worker's level. So, miss me with all that what a boss nigga would do and just give me my shit."

After saying all of that, this nigga's nose flared up and, before I truly knew what was happening, I was being shoved against the wall and this nigga's forearm rested against my throat, pinning me to the wall.

"All that hot shit you spitting would've gotten you a few smacks if I was the lame you trying to paint me out to be. Be happy I'm not a weak ass nigga that gotta hit a bitch to show dominance. Just from the shit you talking, I can tell you ain't never had a nigga try and upgrade you in the sense of putting you up on game. All you see in a nigga is what he can give you financially and materialistically. A bitch nigga could give you all that shit and you would see him as a boss. That's sad, even worse, it says a lot about your take on character. I'm not even gonna hold you. I took you for a bitch who would rather be taught how to make a million instead of being given a million. But, that's my fuck up for putting more stock in a chick than she deserves," he gritted and let me go.

I wanted so badly to slap the fuck outta this nigga and go off, but I couldn't because a bitch was stuck. I watched him go towards what I assumed to be his room and come back with my five stacks and two extra ones.

"Take ya money and dip," he said, tossing the money my way.

"What about the conversation?"

"We had it and you ain't the type of chick I pegged you for, so I ain't got shit for you outside of what I just gave you," he said nonchalantly.

"Wow."

"Yeah wow, why you still standing here? Don't you got dinner with a real boss to go to?"

"First of all, that dinner is with my cousins and, secondly, I want to have that conversation."

"You ain't ready for it lil baby."

"Don't tell me what I'm not ready for."

"Then, you tell me because you're coming off like I got things fucked up."

"You do."

"I don't see how when every assumption I have is created by the energy you give."

"And those assumptions are wrong. I don't need no nigga to give me a million dollars but, if he's gonna hand it over, then I'ma take it. If another dude wants to teach me how to make a million, I'ma entertain that too. Any female to turn down both of those offers is a dumb bitch. I'm not so well off I don't need a handout or can't learn some game. I'ma hustle in every sense of the word until I'm where I need to be."

That must've been the kind of talk he was waiting for because he got up, opened the door for me, and said, "We going to dinner with the fam or nah?"

"I'm going to dinner with *my* family. You might wanna go chop it up with your own."

"You'll be my family in due time."

"In your dreams," I blushed slightly. "Just bring your ass on. We're taking my car."

* * *

"Yo, we gotta take an Uber back to the crib," Jeezy announced once I pulled up to the restaurant and parked.

Cutting my eyes at him, I questioned, "Why would I go back to your crib when I already have my money?"

"We got things to discuss. That money is only gonna last you a hot lil minute and that's if Eddy don't catch up to you first."

"Catch up with me for what? We don't have no business."

"You know I know better than that, right?" he smirked.

"Either way, I'm not going back to your house. We can chill at a Telly or... wait? Why do we need to take an Uber when I got wheels?" I asked, realizing what he had said.

"Man, this shit you're pushing is a death trap. You know it's real when the seat belt is fucked up," he laughed.

"Don't dog my baby out like that. My girl been getting me from point A to point B for a minute. She's never let me down." My 2006 Honda Accord wasn't much, but it got the job done every time.

"That's cool, but you need something better. Something cocaine white with the butter inside."

"Are you gonna foot the bill because I don't have the funds?"

"You'll have them, just play ya cards right."

19

"Mhmm."

Leaving the conversation alone, I walked into Harlem BBQ's ready to fuck some food up. This spot was one of my favorites because the food was bomb and it was a lowkey spot. Smiling at the hostess, I told her who I was looking for and she pointed to a table that was to the far right. Walking over, my smile grew once I was in reach of my cousins.

"Don't y'all look cute!" They were dressed in matching Jersey dresses with uptowns on their feet. Their hair was done perfectly in two ponytails and bamboo earrings that set the outfit on fire.

"You know we don't leave the house looking anything less," Kylie replied, giving me a hug.

Bailey gave me a quick hug after her sister, then turned towards Jeezy and asked, "Who's your friend?"

"Kylie and Bailey, this is Jeezy. Jeezy, these are my baby cousins."

"Nice to meet y'all."

"I would say likewise but, if you're who I think you are, then there's nothing nice about this meeting," Bailey giggled.

"What's she talking about?"

"My reputation must still ring bells in the hood," he smirked, then took a seat.

"Something like that and, before you get cocky, it's mostly bad, not good."

"Niggas are always gonna speak on the bad when speaking down on the next man." Jeezy shrugged.

"And you don't care?"

"No reason to. Once I get back on, those same dudes will be the first in line to kiss my ass. I ain't tripping off fake loyalty."

"Interesting," I mumbled, right before picking up the menu.

Jeezy was so damn mysterious that I found myself wanting to figure him out. He talked hella shit but, if you listened good enough, you could hear all the gems he was dropping at the same time. He was intelligent, which was rare in these bum ass niggas. It was attractive, but what was more attractive was his will to get back on. I knew nothing about Jeezy or his past so, while at dinner, I texted the hood gossip and asked for the 411.

To my surprise, his ass had my hood on lock six months ago. No one really knew why he fell off, and a few of the niggas around that way were just happy he did. It was crazy how you could put niggas on and,, when shit get rough they're the first to laugh at your demise. I was disgusted but, if he wasn't gonna trip, I for damn sure wasn't going to stumble. All I cared about was making sure I got in good, so he could tell Eddy to chill on me. Worker or not, he had to have some type of pull with Eddy. I needed Jeezy to use all his strength because if he didn't, a bitch might not be able to walk around comfortably.

Jeezy

Dinner with Keisha and her people was cool, but I was ready to bounce and get some things figured out.

"You ready to go?" I whispered to Keisha.

"Uh yea," she answered.

"I hope y'all don't think that was a whisper because I heard every word. Y'all a thing now or something?" Kylie smirked.

"When have you known me to be locked down by a nigga? What's that song by Ray J?" Keisha quizzed.

"Cause he ain't gon' tie me down!" they all finished in unison.

"Is that a challenge?"

"And what if it is?" Keisha dared.

"Then, it's accepted."

"Ohhhhh shitttt," sang her cousins.

"Don't hype him. He's not ready for all that I come with. But, you can pay the bill and then we can go." She smiled.

"You got the bill, champ. Break something off that cool seven you got," I smirked, then eased from the table.

Going outside, I leaned against the brick and sparked a blunt. A few seconds later, Kylie and Bailey came walking out of the restaurant, but Keisha wasn't with them.

"Where ya girl at?" I asked.

"You passing?" Bailey asked.

Laughing, I handed her the blunt and waited for my question to be answered.

"You know messing with Keisha isn't going to be easy, right? She has some walls built up, but they're not like your regular bitch's wall. Her shit is iron gated with barbwire," Kylie explained.

"So, she been through some things. Ain't nothing wrong with that."

"Never said it was, but the things she been through isn't your everyday shit. It hits closer to home than she's willing to admit. Just take it easy with my cousin."

"Y'all don't have nothing to worry about. I got her."

"You better," Bailey sassed, passing the blunt back and walking off with her sister in tow.

I continued smoking, thinking about what I was about to get myself into. Keisha wasn't supposed to be a prospect. She was a means to an end that came around at the right time. I wasn't out here looking for a shawty to settle down with because the money was too busy calling. The stunt she pulled was the only reason I took interest. All the fly shit she was kicking intrigued a nigga but, shit, a wet pussy did the same. It wasn't until she popped up at my crib on some gangsta shit that I started to view her differently. She could front all she wanted, but finding my crib wasn't an easy task. She had to know someone who knew someone that might've been related to someone to get my address. The pull-up was a bold move and for her to make it spoke volumes. She wasn't an average female and, when you find a female that can match ya cockiness on some bold shit, you keep her close. Didn't know if the set up I had in mind was gonna turn into a hood romance, but I was gonna keep her as close as I could get her. She might even fuck around and become the pistol to my holster.

"Okay, so where we headed now?" Keisha asked, coming out the restaurant and standing in front of me.

"You said you ain't wanna go back to my place, so you call the move."

"You kinda know my situation, so I can't be seen like that."

"Tell me about what happened."

"For what? Are you gonna save me from the big bad Eddy?"

"You don't seem like the type who needs saving."

"Because I'm not."

"Ight, so tell me what you don't need saving from."

"Fine. So after you left, I acted like I was gonna suck him off and sliced a piece of his dick off."

"Run that back," I said in shock.

"It wasn't a lot; it was like 1/4 of an inch. It's not gonna stop nothing." She shrugged.

"Fuck!" I winced in pain because I felt that shit.

"What happened, you okay?"

"Why you do him like that?"

"Because he's disrespectful. Eddy thinks because he has money, he can treat every female like a hoe. His ugly ass is always trying me and I was tired of it." She shrugged.

"So, what's the plan?"

"I gotta find a new weed connect."

"Cool, but what are you gonna do about Eddy?"

"That's where you come in. Since he's your boss and you're feeling me or whatever, I figured you could put a word in for me."

"What?" I laughed.

"Did I miss something? You work for him, don't you?"

"You got me fucked up."

"I thought since he called you and you came running that..."

My jaw flexed from listening to the bullshit Keisha was talking. I might've not been up, but a nigga wasn't down to the point he had to be runner for the next man.

"I'ma let you have that one, but let's make one thing clear; I don't work for no nigga. I'm my own boss. Anything I do that involves another man is a partnership. Let's not mess things up before they get started."

"I didn't mean anything by it. I just thought-"

"Yo, move on to the next and leave that where it's at."

"Sooo, can you put that word in or... nah?"

"I'm not gon' put a word in, but I got something else for you."

I nodded my head towards her piece of shit she called a car, and she got the hint that it was time to go. On the way to the hotel, I thought about how all of this was gonna play out. All I needed was for Keisha to play the role of a bad bitch and set a few niggas up. The most she had to do was leave a door unlocked or a window open and the rest was gonna be taken care of. Blood was about to spill this summer and I was ready for all the heat that was to come my way. I was tired of these pussy niggas standing on the pedestals that I built. Yeah, my fuck up was the reason I got knocked off, but it damn sure wasn't gonna be the reason I stayed down. I was coming at everyone and snatching every fucking thing.

"So, are we gonna talk because when I get to the spot, I'm taking a shower and going to sleep?"

"You're not gonna kick it with the kid?"

"Hell no. I've spent enough time with your ass. You should be lucky. Strangers usually can't get close to me, let alone get in my car."

"It would've been luck if you saved me from getting in this piece of shit," I joked.

"Keep playing with my baby and we're gonna fight."

"You got hands?"

"What you think?"

"What else you got?"

"An ass so big like the sun!"

"That's ya word cause from what I seen, you got a cupcake," I joked.

Keisha's ass wasn't huge, but it wasn't small either. She had a nice size heart-shaped ass that I wouldn't mind getting behind.

"Stop playing me because I'll have you cuffing... hard."

"Balls and chains haven't been my thing in a long time lil baby. To fly to be on lock."

"Yeah, okay," she smirked, then ran her tongue across her lips. "That's probably why you fell off, didn't have a real bitch holding it down and guiding you."

"Maybe." I shrugged. "Let me switch up the convo before you get ya self in trouble."

"Me in trouble, never. I'll have you licky licky licky licky licky for an hour. I'ma make it rain for you; here's a golden shower. Smell it like a flower; my pussy is a rose. Come a little closer; I wanna fuck your nose."

The way she was quoting Trina had me feeling like she was into some freaky tingz. Working with her was gonna be harder than I thought. The freakier she talked, the sooner I was gonna break her back.

"When's the last time you got fucked?"

"What?"

"You rapped all that freaky shit, then gonna what me. You heard me."

"It's been a minute, but that's by choice."

"Speak on it."

"It's personal."

"And I'ma personal nigga that don't run his mouth. Have faith in me."

The hesitation Keisha was feeling wasn't hard to miss. She was chewing on her bottom lip and constantly glancing my way but not saying anything.

"I didn't mean to overstep. I just wanna get to know you."

"Why?"

"Can't do business with a person I don't know."

"You can't learn everything about me in a matter of hours."

"Who said I'm trying to? We're kicking it for a week or so."

"What? I'm not gonna be stuck with you for a whole week."

"If you want the situation with Eddy to get fixed, then by my side is where you'll be."

"I'll take my chances," she huffed, then turned into the motel parking lot.

"Bet," I told her and stepped out the car.

I'd never been the type to force anyone to do something they didn't wanna do. Lil baby wanted to take her chances; cool, I would just have to figure some other shit out. Either way, I was gonna come out where I needed to be.

Keisha Harper

After showering, I laid across the bed with my phone in hand, ready to text the group chat. I had to tell someone about how I was feeling and the only people I truly trusted were my cousins.

Me: Y'all hoes up?

Kylie: I'm up

Bailey: I'm up but can't talk. Sire in here showing his ass like I won't stab him.

Me: What my boy do now lol

Bailey: I did a pull up and caught him all in a hoe's face. I mean his big headed ass was cheesing and all.

Me: Damnn

Bailey: Exactly

Kylie: Kesh just call me because I'm not about to entertain Bailey's bullshit.

Bailey: Fuck you hoe!

Shaking my head at the last few text messages, I grabbed the tv remote and called Kylie.

"What's going on?"

"Nothing, bored as hell at this hotel."

"Where Jeezy at?"

"I'm not his keeper."

"Could've fooled me."

"Stop it!"

"I'm serious. The two of you were looking real cozy at dinner. I was over there trying to give him that look and his ass wasn't seeing nothing but you."

"What are you talking about?" I laughed. "I just met that damn man. He wasn't tripping off me."

"Denial doesn't look good on you."

"I'm serious, he wasn't sweating me."

"Uh huh, if you say so. But wassup?"

"Remember when I told you I needed to tell y'all something?"

"Yeah."

"Well, I might be in some trouble."

"Lawd, Keisha, what did you do?"

"I went to go reup and Eddy started popping his shit. You know how I get when I feel like someone is trying to play me. His ass was really trying to paint me out to be a hoe. He really took my kindness and tried to flip it. This pussy doesn't pop for every nigga. These lips might keep a conversation going, but it's rare a nigga gets to sample this fountain."

"On gawd!"

"So, I played into it and snipped a little of his tip off."

"You did what?"

"I snipped, snipped the tip and took off with five G's," I laughed.

"Eddy is gonna fuck you up."

"I already know and that's why I'm laying low. I thought Jeezy was gonna be able to put in a word, but he's acting like a bitch."

"How is he supposed to put in a word? That nigga doesn't have no respect in these streets right now."

"I didn't know. All I knew was he was at the spot and Eddy called out to him like he was a lap dog."

"So, why would you think the lap dog can help you?"

"Bitch, I don't know. What I know is he took my money, I got it back and, in my mind, he was gonna help me in my situation."

"So, what happened?"

"He tried to get to know me."

"Uh, that's it?"

"What do you mean that's it? You know I don't allow anyone into my space."

"At what point do you let that go? Off rip, you're goofy for thinking a random ass dude was gonna help you out off the humble. Then, when he tries to get to know you, you show him your barbwire ass fence."

"But, why are you acting like this is new information?"

"I'm not, I'm just tired of it."

"Yeah, well, you can be tired, but I'm protecting myself. I just can't give my dope ass heart away to a nigga that don't deserve it. I don't see the issue anyway. These niggas can go around talking about how they have trust issues and blah blah blah but, when a female says it, they get told to let that shit go. I'm not letting nothing go. When a nigga comes around who proves that he deserves my trust, then he'll have it," I snapped.

I didn't let Kylie say nothing else after that. I hung up after my rant and powered my phone off. Kylie knew better than to come at me like that because she knew what I'd been through and what I was dealing with.

Life hadn't been easy, and it probably never would be. Everything I had, I had to get it on my own because my mom damn sure wasn't going to give it to me. The hood was all my family knew outside of Phour. Phour was the only one who walked away because she was giving the opportunity too; mine never came. All I got was physical and verbal abuse, along with a few other things I choose not to talk about. If you let my mother tell it, I was never supposed to make it on to this green earth and having me was her biggest mistake. That was her favorite dig and I heard it as early as being seven years old. It was like I never lived up to her expectations in private. I say in private because in public, my mother walked around gassing the hell out of me. In public, my mother was proud that I was her daughter and wasn't doing what all these other girls were doing. Soon as it was just us, I was every name in the book who got regular ass whoopings for doing absolutely nothing.

Life was hard and, the older I got, the more I started to resent her. I stayed away from her as much as I could because I didn't want to deal with that bullshit. If I wasn't in Brownsville, then I was at my aunt's house. My auntie Diandra was my heart and there wasn't nothing I wouldn't do for her. Phour didn't know how good she had it. She hated that we all had this *ghetto mentality,* but that same mentality was what made us who we were and why we were some bad bitches. A chick who didn't grow up in the grit would've crumbled at the hands of what I went through. I took everything my mother did on the chin and threw up my wall. On the inside, I was fucked-up emotionally but, on the outside, I was a cool bitch.

"Ugh, I'm bored," I sighed, really not wanting to be in my feelings.

I grabbed the remote and flicked on the tv, hoping to find something to watch but was let down. After that I powered my phone on and went through my texts, looking for a certain somebody to keep me company.

Me: Are you busy?

Jay: Nah wassup.

Me: You wanna come thru?

Jay: Send the addy.

Me: Bring liquor.

Jay: You got green?

Me: Bring that too

Jay: ight.

Just like that, my night was made; wasn't nothing better than getting dick on demand.

* * *

Being awakened by someone pounding on the door wasn't how I wanted to bring in my morning. I had just drifted to sleep a few hours before and was still feeling the effects of the weed, liquor, and dick.

"Who you got coming this way early in the am?" Jay groaned as he rolled out of bed.

I was glad he got up because my ass wasn't moving.

"No one, just make sure you get rid of whoever it is because I'm not in the mood to be bothered."

"Who is it?"

"Jeezy."

His name came smooth through the door and snatched up whatever sleep I had left in me. Now, I'd seen and been around my share of crazy dudes, but Jeezy was on a different level. I got out of bed and headed to the door, ready to give his ass my two cents. Before I could get close enough to open it, Jay had swung the door open and was greeted by the butt of a gun.

"Ahh fuck!" he yelped, holding his nose as the blood came gushing out.

I stood there in complete shock, hoping I was gonna make it out of this situation alive.

"Wassup Keisha? You don't have no words for a nigga?" he questioned, walking in and closing the door behind him.

His words were eerie and the grin he wore was sinister. It was clear he didn't come here to play and even clearer that Jay wasn't going to be any help in this situation.

"What are you doing here Eddy, and why are you using Jeezy's name? I thought yours moved mountains and dropped panties."

"Even when you're looking into the face of death, you're still a smart ass; I gotta respect that," he chuckled.

"To answer your question, my name drops more than panties; it also drops bodies."

"Okay, but that doesn't explain why you came up to my room using another nigga's name," I sassed.

"Using Jeezy's name was to humor myself. When you ducked out with my money, I went over to the window and saw you and him having a conversation. I watched that nigga take the bag from you."

"But, it wasn't what it seemed."

"I think it's exactly how it seems. Nigga, get ya ass the fuck up!" Eddy barked at Jay. He snatched Jay up and placed the gun at his temple and looked me straight in my eye. "You and that nigga set that shit up!" he accused.

"What? I didn't set up anything. I've never met Jeezy until yesterday."

"Bullshit! I saw the eye connection bullshit y'all had going on."

"Eddy, you're tripping."

"Nah, I think I'm stumbling down the right path. You and that nigga from the same hood, right?"

"Yeah, but I don't be over there."

"You must really think I'm stupid. You got one chance to come clean or this nigga's brain is gonna be all around this room."

"Come clean about what Eddy? I'm telling you the truth. Whatever that nigga is on has nothing to do with me. All I did was come to cop my weed like I've always done. You've known me since I was sixteen; do you really think I would play with you like that?"

What happened next played out so slowly that when Jay's lifeless body hit the ground, not a peep escaped my lips. I stood there in horror because in my heart, I knew I was gonna be next.

"I hope that answers your question. Keisha, I'm not fucking playing with you. Tell me the truth or meet the same fate as this nigga."

"I swear to God, I'm telling you the truth. I don't know him. I came to get weed and-"

"And you left with my fucking money and the tip of my dick!"

"Technically, I left the little piece I sliced on the flo... ahhhh!" I cried out in pain.

"Keep talking that bullshit and, next time, it's gonna be more than a slap coming across your face."

"Just tell me what I can do to make this better? I still have all the money. I can give it back to you."

"Go get that!"

"Okay."

I slowly walked towards the closet, making sure to keep my eyes on Eddy. I felt around in the closet for my bag and tossed it in his direction.

"It's all there."

"Take it out the bag."

I did as he said and took the five stacks I stole from him out. The other two stacks I gave to my cousins to put up for me when Jeezy left out of the restaurant.

"I hate that I had to come at you like this Keisha because I like you. You're fine as fuck and that ass is always sitting. I could've made you my main and everything I have could've been yours, but you just had to be one of them bitches who run their mouth and try to outsmart a nigga. Where you fucked up is trying to outsmart the nigga who runs all of Brooklyn. Them blocks ya boy used to run is all me now. You know what that means?"

I shook my head no, and he yelled for me to answer him with words.

"No."

"That shit means it's nothing for me to get ya family touched. See how easy it was for me to find you, Keisha? That nigga Jeezy can't do shit to protect you from me, so you need to give 'em up."

"I can't give up a nigga I don't know. If you have all these damn eyes, then you should know I don't run with this nigga."

"Still talking shit I see. A bitch like you is hardheaded and killing you would be too easy," he smirked. "Bring ya ass over here!"

"Wha... what are you going to do?"

"Shit, it's not what I'm about to do. It's about what you're gonna do for me. Pull my shit down and suck on my balls."

"Excuse me?"

"Bitch, you heard me. Suck my shit or kiss the barrel," he gritted.

"Eddy, I'm-"

Delivering another blow to my face, Eddy spat, "Bitch, I said fucking suck it!"

With my lip quivering, I pulled his stuff down and slurped his balls into my mouth. The tip of his dick was bandaged up and it took everything in me to not squeeze that shit. I continued sucking while his nasty ass moaned and pressed his gun to my forehead.

"Fuck, you gon' make me buss."

I rolled my eyes in disgust but continued on to stay alive. I was on my knees for about twenty minutes when Eddy finally told me I could stand up.

"With a mouth like that, killing you would be an injustice. Fuck, I'ma do it like this; you can keep ya life for the moment. But, every time I ring ya line, you fucking answer and, when I say suck my dick, you do that shit. You hear me?"

"I hear you," I mumbled.

"Speak the fuck up."

"I hear you, Eddy," I all but yelled.

"Good. Make sure ya boy come by and clean this mess up and, when he does, let him know his days are limited."

"I already told you I don't run with that-"

Instead of smacking me like he did the first two times, Eddy chose to punch me repeatedly. I guess not killing me wasn't good enough and he felt damage had to be done. I took the pain, never yelling for help and refusing to let a tear fall. When he was done, he spit on me and demanded I tell Jeezy that he was coming for him next. After he left, I struggled to stand up because of the pain I was in. Jay's body just laid there, and I couldn't take my eyes off it. I single-handedly got someone killed and was degraded for standing up for myself. This was the highest form of humiliation and I wasn't just going to take it. By no means was I a killer or even about *that* life but, when provoked, the ugliest side of you had a tendency of coming out.

Jeezy

"Yessssss Jeezy, just like that. I'm about to cum all over this diiiiick," Issa cooed.

Soon as she said that, her walls started pulsating and her thick cream became visible whenever I slid out the pussy. I smacked her ass and started pounding the cheek. Issa kept up with my speed and made her ass clap more than it already was.

"Fuck!" I groaned, tightening up.

I got a few more pumps in before pulling out and cumming on her ass. She fell against the pillow and I eased from the bed, heading into the bathroom.

"Don't forget to get the rag!" I heard her call out.

I cleaned myself up, grabbed a rag for her and tossed it at her when I went back in the room.

"Um… what am I supposed to do with this?"

"You asked for it, right?"

"Yeah."

"Ight, then handle ya shit."

"You can't be serious," she huffed.

"What, you want a towel so you can shower?"

"So, you're not gonna clean me off?"

"Hell no. You're the one who wanted to switch up what we had going on. I was cool letting my seeds off in ya garden."

"I bet you were!" she sassed. "You know, Jeezy, I'm starting to get real tired of your shit."

"Heard that before."

"And that's how true it is. How do you figure it's cool for you to be nutting in me without giving me any type of commitment?"

"Cause that 'no commitment' shit was ya terms. You didn't want to take shit seriously."

"Because I was trying to focus on school. I'm bussing my ass to become a neurosurgeon. I can't mess up my plans by being tied down."

"Damn, I'ma anchor now?" I laughed.

Issa just didn't understand the damage she was doing to me. Hurt wasn't a feeling that hit me easily; it took a lot for a muthafucker to get under my skin. When I met Issa, all that changed and I fell for her hard. She had me wrapped around her finger and everyone in the hood knew it. My first love was what she was and my last was what she was supposed to be. I wanted it all with her and, for a hot second, she wanted it with me too. Out of the blue, she switched up on me and wanted to focus on her studies. I respected her decision and still held it down. I wasn't out here cheating or nothing, just focusing on the money.

When she became too busy, I did the manly thing and allowed her to set the terms for how things would play out between us, that's how badly I wanted her in my life. I saw a future in Issa but, as time went on, feelings started to fade and I was over the bullshit. No matter what, I was gonna have love for her because of the history, but that was it. As fucked up as it sounded, the only reason I was still in contact was because the pussy was easy and I ain't have the time to scout new pussy.

"You know what I mean. You also know what it means for me to be with you. Everything you have going on with this street shit is a lot and I can't be worried about you while trying to focus on school."

"You don't have to explain cause I'm cool. The conversation came up because you wanna question why I'm not cleaning you off."

"Whatever. I'ma go shower."

"You do that."

She sucked her teeth and went into the bathroom while I grabbed my phone. Three missed calls from a number I didn't know caught my attention. The person didn't leave a message and they ain't text. I deleted them out my call log and went to text Casper. He had a spot he wanted me to check out and I told him I was game. Before I could send that text off, the random ass number started calling. I answered but waited for the person on the other end to speak first.

"Jeezy?" the soft voice spoke. "Please say this is you. I need to see you. It's Keisha."

"Yo."

"Yo?" she questioned. From her tone, I knew her face was scrunched up and her big ass lips were pressed together.

"Yo? Did you not just hear me say I need to see you?"

"Yeah, but what that gotta do with me? Could've sworn you said you're good on your own."

"I did, but that was before the circumstances got crucial. Are you busy? If so, I can come to you; it's not an issue."

She was being her regular snappy self, but her confidence was gone.

"I'm caught up with someone right now, but I can hit you back in an hour or two."

"That's not gonna work. I need to see you *now*."

"Chill with the attitude cause you need me."

"Correction, we need each other. I'll be waiting at the Holiday Inn room 305."

"Shit, don't hold ya breathe," I snickered, then hung up.

"Who was that?" Issa asked, standing in the doorway of the bathroom. Her birthday suit glistened underneath the lights. Her nipples were at attention and her hand kept grazing over her pussy.

"Where ya clothes at?"

"In the bathroom where they belong. I figured I would feed you a little snack before you run off to whatever bitch that was."

"Is that jealousy I hear?"

"Never that baby. Those hoes you fuck with could never take my spot. I'm the end and the beginning," she smirked.

"You sound real confident about that shit."

"I am. Is there a reason I shouldn't be?"

"Feel how you want. I'm Gucci on that snack tho."

"Since when?"

"Since I have something else to do. Get dressed, so I can dip."

"Oh, now I have to leave when you do?"

"Yeah. I been meaning to take that key back anyway. You got ten minutes and leave my shit on the nightstand," I told her and headed for the other bathroom to shower.

Issa had this whole situation fucked up. She wasn't the end and the beginning to nothing I had going on. I was good on her and, in a minute, this sex shit was gonna come to an end. Other shit was starting to come into play and Keisha's phone call confirmed all of that. If I had to guess, Eddy paid her a visit and words were exchanged, probably with my life being on borrowed time or some bullshit like that. Niggas like Eddy loved playing the intimidation game. He talked big shit and would come at the dudes he knew weren't gonna take him to war. He was as pussy as they come, and that made shit ten times easier for me because dealing with pussy ain't never been something I shied away from.

* * *

"Fuck taking you so damn long. Open this muthafucker up!" I barked, banging on Keisha's room door.

After that first call, she called me two more times and texted me about ten. Eddy really did a number on her cause patience wasn't a fucking virtue at this point.

"What you looking at? Am I banging on your door?" I gritted at some white dude who was eyeing me suspiciously.

He hurried into his room, and I continued banging. A few seconds later, Keisha came opening the door but peeked her head out before letting me.

"Do you need to talk or what?" I asked her.

"Yeah but I just need to make sure no one-"

"I ain't got no one with me," I assured her, then pushed the door open.

Man, soon as that shit opened wide enough, I saw what had her ass shook. I pushed her into the room and slammed the door behind me.

"What happened?" I asked.

"I was... I... Jay... Eddy..."

"Get it together Keisha. That mumbling shit isn't telling me nothing I need to know."

"I'm just a little shaken up and uh… scared," Keisha sighed, running her hand over her face.

"I get ya emotions are all over the place right now, but you got a body in this bitch and the A.C. isn't on. Do you know what that means?"

"No."

"It means that funky ass smell you got in this bitch is about to get a lot stronger. I can help you, but I need you to run shit down to me. What happened."

"I was here with my friend Jay when Eddy came knocking on the door. He said he was you, so I didn't think nothing of it. Jay opened the door before I could get there and Eddy walked in, going off. I tried to tell him that you and I weren't working together, but he had his mind made up. He killed Jay, beat me and made me... made me suck his balls."

"Damn."

Hearing that last part fucked me up. I didn't care about ole boy Eddy killed, but the way he handled Keisha was grimy. I heard stories about how Eddy gave it up when it came to females; I just never believed it. It was hard to when he never had the same energy for dudes. The niggas he ran with was the muscle and he was just the mouth. Off the strength of Keisha being a female, I was gonna make sure Eddy got what he deserved.

"What am I going to do Jeezy? He told me whenever he calls, I better answer and fall through."

"Do you trust me?"

"Hell no!"

"Then, what was the point in calling me? What we got going on can only be dealt with if trust is involved. You need me and I'ma need you."

"How can I trust someone I don't know?"

"I'm about to get rid of a dead body for you. If that doesn't earn me an ounce of trust, then I don't know what to tell you."

She said nothing, but I could tell she was thinking about what I said. Her not putting a hundred in me was understandable; yet, for this to work, she was gonna have to come up off 20 or something. This whole thing wasn't gonna work if there was no type of trust involved. Everything from this point on was about to get real illegal.

45

Keisha Harper

T he right words couldn't find me because I'd never seen or been in anything like this. Yeah, gun shots were a normal thing where I grew up, but I wasn't seeing bodies fall on a daily. I for damn sure wasn't getting threatened to the point I had to degrade myself. This whole thing was out of the norm and putting my trust in Jeezy was starting to seem even more unusual.

"So, wassup, can I have faith in you? Or is it gonna be one sided?"

Again, I couldn't answer him because he was asking for the one thing I didn't give or put too much on when it came to anyone. Everyone in my life didn't know much about what I had going on. Each person knew a little of this and a little of that, but no one knew everything and the never would. If my own momma couldn't be fully trusted, then no one in this world could. I fucked with everyone at arm's length with the exception of my cousins but, even with that, the information they got was vague.

"I'm not trying to stress you or nothing, but we don't have time to sit here looking dumb. You gotta make a decision and you need to do it now. We either gonna handle this and get back at Eddy, or I'ma walk outta this bitch and let you deal with whatever consequences might come."

That right there got my mouth to moving real quick.

"That's crazy," I snickered, shaking my head. "If I don't give you the answer you're looking for, then you're just gonna dip and leave me with a mess that ain't mine to clean."

"I don't know this nigga. He's your people and that makes this your mess."

"He's only dead because of your dumb ass! Eddy killed him because he thought I was lying about us knowing each other!" I shouted.

"Again, your people your problem."

"How can you say that when Eddy has beef with *you*? Whatever odds y'all have happened way before I came into the picture. So, this body is on me as much as it's on you."

"Look, there's no point in going back and forth because I'm willing to help. I just need to know you ain't gon' turn on me. This shit ain't gonna be pretty and, if things get fucked up, we looking at years in a cage. I'm not an animal and don't plan on getting treated like one, so there's nothing to worry about on my end."

"So, the worry falls on me?"

"Fuck yea. You talk a lot of shit, but you ain't close to being about that life."

"I can handle it."

"For the moment. When your back is against the wall, can you stand ten toes down with your head held high?"

"I could tell you yeah, but you won't believe it. The same way trust don't come easy for me, it doesn't come easy for you. Getting rid of this body for me gives you leverage. I don't blame you cause I would do the same. What I don't appreciate is you putting this on me as if I should yes to everything you say. I don't like you and I'm sure you don't like me; the only thing keeping this thing together is the need for revenge. Long as I'm the one to kill Eddy, then we good."

"You ain't a killer."

"Don't have to be. It takes a second to pull the trigger and that's all I need."

"That shit can change you."

"I'm already changed. Are we gonna clean this up or keep talking about me and my feelings?"

"You got it lil baby," he smirked.

Before we could do anything, someone started knocking on the door. I damn near pissed myself when I heard the person say it was the manager. Just like that, I saw my life flash before my eyes and what I saw told me that jail wasn't a place I needed to be. I rushed over to the window to see what a third floor jump would be like.

"I know ya ass ain't thinking about jumping?" Jeezy gritted, snatching me back.

"What else am I supposed to do because jail is out the equation?"

"Go flirt with the nigga and tell him everything is straight."

"What?"

"Ya ass can't flirt or something?"

"Why won't you flirt with him? He might be gay."

"He can be what he wants. I like pussy."

"Ugh!" I rolled my eyes at him and went over to the door trying to be as normal as possible.

"Hey." I smiled, opening the door and sliding out.

"Is everything okay Ms. Harper? We got a disturbance complaint about someone banging on the door."

"Oh yes, we're fine. My... um... my boyfriend just came by and he was a little upset about an argument we got into earlier. I handled the situation."

"Are you sure because your face looks pretty bad? Did he put his hands on you? I can call the police if you need me to."

"No... no, everything is fine. These are just love taps."

As soon as that came out my mouth, I wanted to slap myself for how stupid I sounded.

"I don't mean to overstep but, Ms. Harper, there is no such thing as love taps and you shouldn't be telling yourself there is. If you need help, I'm willing to help you."

"I don't need help. I'm fine!" I yelled a little too loudly. "I'm sorry. I'm a little on edge with everything I have going on."

"No need to apologize. I have a sister who went through the same thing. If you need anything while you're staying here, please let me know."

"Um... the only thing is that I have to go and run an errand, but I don't want to walk out the front. Is it okay if I go out the back entrance?"

"When will you be leaving?"

"Within twenty minutes or so. Me and a friend of mine have a bag full of clothes and other things that I need to take to my mother's house."

"The back door is fine. I'll let the person at the front desk know."

"Okay, thank you so much."

"It's nothing. Be safe Ms. Harper."

"I will, thank you."

I slipped back in the room, and Jeezy already had Jay in a big ass garbage bag.

"You don't waste time, do you?"

"Not when there's no time to waste. You handled that?"

"Yeah, we can leave out the back door but you're gonna have to put more stuff in that bag."

"I'll put the blanket in there. Do you know if this place has cameras?"

"Of course they do. It might not be a fancy hotel, but it's not the hoe spot either."

"We need that tape."

"That's all you."

"You sure you want me to handle it because asking nicely isn't how I'ma go about it."

"We're in a public fucking place. Why do you think killing someone is the answer?"

He shrugged, and I shook my head.

"We can get the tape after we get something to clean up the blood."

"I got someone coming to handle it."

"Who?"

"Why?"

"Because this is my ass hanging on the line too."

"A chem student. Don't trip, he's trustworthy."

"I still want to know who he is," I spat.

"You can meet him when he get here. Get ya purse cause we moving this nigga now"

"Give me a second to fix my face. I didn't think it was bad because you didn't mention it, but that manager was ready to fuck you up behind it," I said and went off into the bathroom.

Gazing at my face in the mirror, I was disgusted. Never in my life had my face ever looked as bad as it did. Underneath my eye was small cuts and bruises. My lip was swollen and my nose was red. There was no way I could be out looking like this. Once the twins got wind of how I was looking, they would be ready for war. I couldn't have that and I didn't want them in this drama. Everything that happened with Eddy was on me and that's why it was up to me to off his ass.

"Yo, you ready?" Jeezy questioned, knocking.

"Give me a second."

I threw on my oversized sunglasses and told myself that I was still that bitch. Strutting out of the bathroom, I snapped my fingers and told Jeezy to bring his ass on and let's get this over with.

* * *

A few hours or so later, we were pulling back up to the motel and I felt like I was traumatized. Today had been a long day, but what messed me up the most was watching Jeezy dispose of Jay's body. Jay and I weren't a thing; it was just a sex. When he needed it, I gave it up and vice versa. He was a cool lil daddy and that's why I rocked with him. He wasn't into all the street stuff and kept to himself as far as I knew. What happened to him was tragic and he didn't deserve it, the same way he didn't deserve being thrown in a fire to be nothing more but dust. The worse part of it all was his family would never know what happened to him. They would never be able to say goodbye or have that sense of peace knowing he was in a better place. Tears began falling from my eyes just thinking about it.

"You ight?" Jeezy asked, looking my way.

"I'm cool," I lied.

"Why you have to lie? That tough shit is cute until it ain't."

"All I said was I'm cool."

"Yeah, but you're not. It's okay to show emotion Keisha. Being on two instead of ten doesn't make you less than."

"I'm not worried about being less than. I'm scared that if I let these emotions in and take over, I'll never be able to bounce back. The snappy comebacks keep me safe."

"You don't have to play it safe with me."

He leaned over and slid my glasses off. I turned away and he brought my face right back.

"Don't hide because you're a little bruised up. It doesn't take away from your beauty."

"You think I'm beautiful?" I whispered.

"I think you're ugly as fuck, but I'm sure some nigga out there will appreciate what you look like," he laughed.

"You got fucking nerve calling me ugly. I'm the finest thing that's ever been this close to you. This face is beautiful and my kitty is just as pretty. Stop playing like you don't know my body," I boasted.

"Just had to get you back on ya shit. I know things seem fucked up right now, but everything is gonna be cool."

"It better be because I just witnessed you commit a crime," I smirked and stepped out the car.

"I ain't worried bout that. You won't fuck over ya baby daddy." He grinned.

"Nigga, you out here getting these hoes pregnant?" a skinny Jeezy lookalike laughed.

"Fuck no. It's rubbers until I die and, if I swim raw, then it's plan B."

"Um, you missed the part where you tell this ignorant fuck that I'm not a hoe, let alone a bitch you're fucking."

"Oh, she sassy as fuck," Dude smirked, then rubbed his hand together like Birdman. "What's ya name sweetheart?"

"Bye!" I spat, smacking my lips.

I turned my back to him and waited for Jeezy to finish whatever conversation this was gonna lead to.

"Yo, where you find her? She looking like wifey, attitude and all."

"You don't wanna mess with her mean ass. She likes pussy."

"Shit, me too. We can make it a three-way thing."

"Don't let this ugly nigga gas you because no pussy has ever touched these lips."

"She cold forreal."

"She ight," Jeezy said. "You ready to take care of that for me?"

"You know it's nothing. Give me the room key and two hours."

"Keisha, give him ya key."

"Who is he?"

"My bad beautiful, the name is Jake but you can call me Poppa."

"Not even in your dreams," I said before tossing him the key card. "Don't steal nothing of mine either."

"I'm not even like that. Ya panties will be there when you get back," he laughed then took off.

"Is that really your brother?"

"Yeah," Jeezy chuckled.

"I feel bad for your mother."

"Talk shit about whoever and whatever, but don't speak on my dukes," he said in a dry tone.

"Relax, it was a joke," I huffed.

"Kesh, I don't give a fuck what it was. Chill on it cause I've fucked up muthafuckers for less."

The grittiness in his voice let me know he wasn't playing and, after getting slapped around by one nigga, I wasn't in the mood to throw hands with another.

"I didn't mean anything by it. I was just-"

"Long as you leave dukes out of it, we cool. No need to further explain."

"Uh… okay."

"Stay here. I'ma go get that tape."

"You sure you don't want me to come with you?"

"Nah. I'll be back."

He walked off, and I stood there feeling bad for coming out my mouth. I wasn't trying to be offensive; I just thought with the both of them, his mother had a lot to deal with. Pushing the issue to the side, I started walking up the block to get some food. I hadn't eaten all day and was starving. To try and be nice, I was gonna get Jeezy and his brother something too. It was the least I could do with all that they were doing for me.

James 'Jeezy' Brown

The way I flipped on shawty was probably wrong and a nigga should've apologized, but that wasn't gon' happen. There were only two things on this earth I didn't play about. My dukes was number one and Jake was the second. Harm coming to those two could cause a war that niggas weren't ready for. Keisha was joking and I knew that; I just didn't appreciate the negative undertone. Ms. Jazmyn Brown was my heart in the flesh. Like every other single mother, she broke her back to make sure her kids were straight. She gave up everything for us. I'm talking fucked up nails, toes, hair and clothes, just so we could be good. Jake and I walked around in name brand everything while my duke kept it simple and hit up drift shops. She knew what it was like to grow up in Brooklyn without having much. Muthafuckers out here were brutal and, to protect her kids, she went without. Repaying her was the goal but the debt was never truly gonna be paid. She was owed the world and I would give my last breath to make sure she had it.

"Mhmm, they don't make 'em like you around my way." A female wearing a security guard outfit smiled. I licked my lips and took her in. She wasn't the prettiest female to walk the earth, but I swore she had the fattest ass. Her hips from the front looked wide as fuck so, when she turned slightly and I caught a glimpse of that ass, I knew this was gon' be an easy mark.

"That's cause a nigga is one of one."

"Is that ya word?"

"Whatchu think?"

"I think you're roaming around an area you shouldn't be in. Let me show you back to your room and you can continue telling me about your one of one status."

"That would be the move if I wasn't caught up in a jam. My ole lady is actually staying here."

"Umph," she huffed.

"Relax cause things are done after what happened. I caught her hoe ass fucking the next nigga and I lost it. Straight beat the shit outta her and now she talking about going to the cops."

"Damn. That's crazy."

"You don't know the half. I fucked her up in the hallway and I know y'all got footage."

"And if the cops come this way, we gonna have to hand it over too."

"Facts."

"So, why are you roaming around the security office? I know you're not trying to run up and take the tape?"

"Come on baby, how you gonna offend me like that? Do I look like the type to run up and snatch what I want?"

"Hell fucking yea."

"Wooow!" I played hurt. "I'm offended."

"Don't be, that's just my type," she purred. "I'll tell you what. I'm a little backed up and in need of a release, if you know what I mean. Scratch my kitty and I'll give you the tape."

"Just like that?"

"Just like that. You're too fine and, from the way you talk, I know you got a little motion to ya ocean."

"We can fuck, but I'ma need to know you're clean."

"Clean as a whistle. I can show you, give me a second."

She disappeared into the security room then came back with a piece of paper. She passed it to me and, sure enough, she had a clean bill of health.

"Whatchu you doing carrying std test results around?"

"I don't carry it. I signed into my health portal and printed it. Never know who you might come across that you wanna get down with."

"You wild," I chuckled.

"Mhmm, you don't know the half but you're gonna find out. Follow me."

I followed her into the security office and fucked her silly. Shawty's face was hit, but her pussy was lethal. She was doing all types of crazy shit with her coochie muscles. If this fuck was on regular circumstances, I might've kept her on standby. Since it was a run and done, I got her off, grabbed my tape and dipped. Walking towards my car, I didn't see Keisha.

"Where you at?" I asked after she answered the phone.

"Up the block at the diner. I was hungry."

"Ight, I'm on my way."

She wasn't far, but I wasn't bout to walk a damn place. I jumped in my whip and pulled up to the diner in five minutes flat.

"You order me something?" I grabbed a seat at the counter and snatched a fry from her plate.

"I was going to but, when you didn't call after ten minutes, I figured I'll order you something when I was on my way back. You can just have this tho," she smacked, then pushed her plate towards me.

"What's wrong?" She was still rocking them oversized glasses, but they did nothing to hide her attitude.

"Nothing."

"Then, why you pass me ya plate like that?"

"You obviously wanted it more than I did."

"What I do?"

"If you have to ask then-"

"We're not about to do the whole back and forth thing. It was cute at first, but it's getting played out. If I did some shit you ain't like, then say that."

"How would you feel if I came from God only knows where and put my hands in your food?"

"That's my bad, but you know where I was at."

"Do I? You went to go get that tape a little over an hour ago, so I'm sure you got into a little more than a computer system."

"If I did, what you care?"

"I don't. The point is don't put your nasty hands in my food."

"You got it lil baby," I told her with my hands up.

"I know I do, and you can order me another basket of fries and a milkshake."

"Bet. Let's move to a booth."

"Okay."

Grabbing her hand, I helped her off the stool, snatched up the fries and followed her to a booth. I started to sit next to her, then nixed the idea when I saw her look at me crazy. I chuckled and sat across from her.

"Can we have a conversation?"

"Isn't that what started the whole back and forth thing between us?"

"Not a convo about the bs, but a conversation to get to know each other."

"I mean, do we really have to?"

"We're gonna be spending a lot of time together. We gotta at least be friends."

"Friends?"

"Yeah. That's all I got room for; plus, you're not my type."

"Oh shit, we lying to each other now? I'm everyone's type." She smiled.

"Cocky, but I see why. Back to the convo tho, you gonna let me get to know you?"

"I guess. What you wanna know?"

"What's ya name?"

"Keisha."

"Full name."

"You the feds?"

"If I was, your ass going straight to jail after what I witnessed today."

"So annoying," she giggled. "Keisha Jazlyn Harper. What's yours?"

"James Brown."

"What?!" she hollered out in laughter.

"Chill on my shit," I chuckled.

Man, I hated my name because everyone had the same reaction when they found out what it was. Dukes was tripping heavy naming me that bullshit.

"Why? Just why?"

"You let her tell it, she just knew I was gonna be able to sing and dance as good as him.

"Well, can you?"

"Can I what?"

"Sing and dance."

"Yeah," I smirked.

"You're lying!"

"I'm deadass."

"Let me hear something then."

"That's on reserve for my wife and daughter."

"Mhmm."

"What's your favorite color?" I questioned, keeping the conversation going.

"Orange and don't try to be slick and not order my food."

"I got you right now."

I waved the waitress over and ordered her food and got a few things for myself. We continued the conversation and I learned more about lil baby than I thought I would. She was silly as fuck on the low but stayed guarded to protect her from whatever in her past haunted her. She was a cool lil vibe.

Keisha Harper

L ooking around the motel room, it was like Jay's body was never there.

"So, what you think?" he asked.

"I don't wanna say I like it because you shouldn't have had to come clean up, but I'm impressed," I answered honestly.

"Does that mean I can get ya number?"

"Nigga, move around. You'll have that in your account in a week or two," Jeezy said, pushing him towards the door.

"Always hating on a young playa," he scuffed. "Keisha, get my number from his hating ass if you change ya mind."

"Okay," I laughed as he left.

"Don't encourage that shit. Pack ya stuff, so we can dip."

"Why are we leaving?"

"Cause Eddy been by here and he don't need to be popping up on you again."

"Well, I don't want to go home, so what am I supposed to do? I can't bring that type of drama to my momma's door."

"You still live with ya mom?"

"And?"

"Yo, relax, cause it was just a question. You can come crash with me."

"I'll pass. I wouldn't want to step on any of your hoe's toes."

"Don't have any for you to step on and it wasn't a debate."

"You don't tell me what to do."

"I'ma let you think that, but we out." He shrugged "I'll wait for you in the car."

"I can drive myself."

"That's cool. You can follow me over there and I'll leave you with my key. I got something I need to deal with."

"Okay."

Jeezy walked out the door, and I started packing my stuff. I didn't have much here because I didn't plan on staying for long. It was gonna be a few days tops, and then my life was going to go back to normal. Or at least that's what I thought. Sadly, things took a bad turn and, now, I had to deal with the consequences. As I stuffed everything in my bags, I let a few tears slip for Jay. No matter what it took, I was going to make sure his death wasn't in vain.

Starring at myself in the mirror, I promised those tears would be the last ones I cried until this whole thing was over and done with. I couldn't be a sad bitch on a mission. I needed the dark to dim my light and for the cold to overcome my warmth. I was about to become a whole new bitch, one muthafuckers weren't gonna wanna see.

* * *

"You can sleep in the guest bedroom at the end of the hall. Don't go in my shit and don't touch my shit. Other than that, you're good to do whatever," Jeezy told me as we walked in to his place.

"Can we at least go food shopping tomorrow? I don't know what you survive on, but I can't live off dust."

"You got it," he laughed.

"Cool," I said, then remembered I needed him to do something for me. "Here, take these and burn them please."

"Smart girl. If you need anything while I'm out, let me know and I'll pick it up for you."

I nodded my head and headed off towards the guest room. It was bare as hell with nothing in it but a bed and a flat screen.

"This nigga got a whole loft but keeps it empty," I mumbled.

I laid across the bed and started going through my phone. I texted the twins back, letting them know I was good. They tried to get me to come out, but I wasn't feeling it. We texted for a few more before Phour was calling my phone.

"What do I owe the pleasure of this phone call?" I sassed.

"Why does it always have to be an attitude with you? When you don't hear from me, it's a problem. When you do hear from me, you give me attitude. Maybe I should leave your ass alone."

"It's not even that serious. Wassup?"

"I was just calling to check on you."

"I'm... I'm fine," I lied.

"You know I can still tell when you're lying, right?"

"I'm fine Alicia!"

"Don't call me that and raising your voice isn't going to convince me. What trouble did you get yourself in now?"

"Why do you always think the worse when it comes to me? Maybe I just had a bad day or something."

"When does Keisha Harper ever have a bad day?"

"My life isn't perfect Phour."

"Never said it was but it damn sure isn't difficult. You have no goals, standards or aspirations, making your day by day easy as hell. What's the hardest part of your day? Trying to figure out what dude is gonna get your attention? Or is it finding a bitch to slap?"

"Wow!"

"Don't sound shocked because you know it's the truth. I love you and my sisters, but all three of y'all have to do better. The hood never loved a soul and, the longer y'all keep that ghetto mentality, the longer it's going to be for good to come to you."

"I have to go," I whispered, holding back the tears.

"Just think about what I said and, if you need help, I'm here to help you."

"Whatever," I spat, hanging up the phone.

I always knew Phour thought I was less than but to hear her say it made everything different. She swore because I wasn't out here chasing a degree that I had no dreams. School wasn't everything and working for a white man for damn sure wasn't a goal I wanted to have. Yeah, I played the hood and pushed my weed, but that was only because I couldn't settle on what I wanted to do. I was only 23. I had a few years to get it together and figure things out. Until those years hit, I planned on enjoying my life now instead of in old age. All in all, Phour was a bitch and her words shouldn't have gotten to me. I knew my potential, the same way I knew something great was going to come knocking on my door the moment I was ready to receive.

James 'Jeezy' Brown

few days had passed by and a nigga was ready to get back out and play the streets. Playing the crib was cool for the first twenty-four hours. Keisha and I hit up the supermarket and she made sure I had breakfast, lunch and dinner. It was cute, but doing the same things every day was tiring. Keisha was the reason I hadn't made any plays yet. Her face was taking some time to heal and, like a true female, she wasn't going anywhere until it was back to normal. I told her ass to slap some makeup on to cover up the bruises, but she wasn't trying to hear it. She claimed she didn't do the makeup thing because her skin was sensitive. I thought that was bs because every chick was out here wearing makeup. Instead of forcing her to do what I wanted, I let her take control.

It was going on day eight of being on lock down and I couldn't take it anymore. The longer we took to get things in motion, the better the chance that this whole shit wasn't going to work. Eddy was a lazy muthafucker, but he always got busy eventually. Before he could put word out, I wanted to have things in place. When it all boiled down, Eddy was gonna be the one who needed to come and see me.

"Wake up champ, it's game day!" I yelled, snatching the covers off Keisha.

"Nigga, are you fucking crazy!" she spat, trying to get the blanket back.

"Damn," I whispered and adjusted myself.

Keisha was beautiful and there was no denying that. Her naked brought a whole different kind of beauty to the table. Her complexion was so rich and deep that it glistened underneath the sunrays peeking in through the window. I licked my lips, wondering if her skin tasted how it looked, chocolate. Breasts sat up nicely and her nipples were hard and big, just how I liked them. The kitty was hairless and her ass was bigger than I thought. I wasn't trying to be a perv or nothing, but I caught a hard-on admiring her beauty.

"Do you fucking mind?!"

"My bad I ain't..." I couldn't even apologize cause I was so caught up.

"Just get out please!"

I threw the blanket at her and left out. I sat on the couch waiting for her to grace me with her presence. I gave her ass about twenty minutes before I grew restless and went back towards the room.

"Why are you back in here?" She smacked her lips and rolled her eyes.

"We have moves to make."

"I think that *we* should be replaced with *you*. I haven't been home in a week and I need to show face before my cousins put out an amber alert."

"We can do that after we get to business."

"I'm not really in the mood to handle *business*." She shrugged and pushed pass me.

Keisha was really trying my patience with her bullshit. A week had already been lost and we couldn't afford to fuck up any more days.

"Where you think you're going?" I questioned, snatching her back by the arm.

"Get your hands off me."

"Or what?" I taunted.

Smirking, she thought she was slick and tried kicking me in the balls. I backed up just in time, then pinned her little ass against the wall. I rested my front against hers and locked eyes with her.

"This the second time you've put hands on me. Is beating women your thing?"

"Snatching you up doesn't come close to me putting my hands on you. What that pussy nigga did to ya face is beating on you and laying hands. If you want me to get gully, I can do that. Just know when it's all said and done, you won't be alive to tell a soul who did it.

"Is that supposed to scare me?" she laughed. "You might wanna come up with a new strategy because my life has already been threatened, or did you forget? Nothing about you scares me and it never will. So with all of that being said, take your nasty ass hands off me."

"Who do you think someone is playing with ya ass? Whatever nigga you were fucking with before got ya head all fucked up. The sun doesn't rise and set on ya ass. I do what the fuck I want when I wanna do it. That includes me taking my hands off you," I snarled. "You got shit all the way fucked up. We got work to do and ya ass wanna sit up in bitches' faces like we got time-"

Slap!

"Nigga, watch ya mouth when you're speaking on my family!" she barked. "You think I don't know we have stuff to do? Before I can even wrap my mind around the

71

things I'm about to do, I need my family to know I'm good. I also need them to get out of Gravesend until this thing is over. You might not care about that nigga coming for yours, but I'll be damn if he touches mine. So, again, I'm gonna show my face, and you can either come along or you can go and do whatever you need to."

Letting her go, I ran my hand over my face and gave in. "Hurry the fuck up and get dressed. We can shoot to Coney and see ya peeps. Right after, we're handling the first nigga on the list. He lives around that way, so it's cool."

"I knew you'd see things my way," she smirked and walked off.

I shook my head because this shit was gonna be a headache. I was trying to approach the whole situation from a friend aspect. She needed a friend to talk to about this shit and I was willing to be that. I tried getting to know her but only got so far. She opened up a little but, when the serious topics came up, she shut right down. That shit was lame because she was game to watch movies, chat about bullshit and just vibe out with the kid but couldn't see pass that. The more time I spent, I was starting to see that she had a problem with letting a nigga take the wheel. Keisha wasn't gonna have a choice but to let go of control because I played the lead role. She needed to get with the program quick because we had a short window of two weeks to get this shit done. After that, the plan was to dip off to Philly and lay low for a month or two. When we touched back in Gravesend and Bedstuy, it was gonna be minute, and my takeover would begin.

* * *

"I guess I see why your ass been missing in action for a whole week," Kylie huffed, then rolled her eyes at me.

"We got a problem?" I asked her.

"Nigga, I don't know, you tell me? What I do have a problem with is Keisha going missing for days and then popping up with you right by her side."

"What's wrong with that?"

"What you mean? You're watching her like a fucking hawk. Y'all not an item, so you shouldn't be that invested."

"You funny," I chuckled.

"No, the only thing funny is where you're going to end up if you got my cousin in some bullshit."

"Kylie, chill out because he doesn't have me in anything," Keisha defended.

"Then, why do we have to leave home? I know this nigga got you caught up in something and, if something happens to you, I'ma kill his ass myself."

"Lil baby, get ya people. She talking real reckless."

"If it's a problem, you handle me so I can slice ya stupid ass the fuck up."

"Kylie, can you stop because you're doing the most? I got into some trouble on my own. I already told you about it, so I don't know why you're tripping. I'm handling it with the help of Jeezy."

"What can he do for you that I can't? Let me help you, Kesh. I don't trust his ass."

"All I need from you is to make sure that my mom, auntie, Bailey and you are safe in A.C."

"I can get us there, but who is going to pay for that? You know how our mother's get when they're near a casino. I don't have money for that and I'm not dealing with their attitudes because of it."

73

"I can send you some money for them. I just need for y'all to get ghost today."

"I wish you would just tell me the real, so I can help."

"There's nothing you can do and everything I've said is the truth. Please just do as I asked."

"Okay but make sure you check in with me daily. I don't trust this beady eye muthafucker, so be careful."

"Always."

Keisha and her cousin shared a hug before she took off back in her building. Turning towards me, Keisha shot daggers in my direction.

"Fix ya eyes cause I ain't do shit," I said before she could get a word out.

"Do you always gotta come outta ya mouth? Show some respect every once in a while."

"Respect is shown when it's given, not off the strength of someone wanting me to give it. Shawty was coming at me sideways and I sent her ass the same energy. Knock her before you try and snap on me."

"Ohhhhhhh," she sang, laughing sarcastically. "I guess if we're going by that logic, I should disrespect the fuck outta ya momma huh?"

"You're reaching but, if you want to test those waters, be my guest."

I already told Keisha how I was giving it up behind mine. If she wanted to take that risk because I said something back to her cousin, then fuck it.

"You know what… I'm not about to do this with your stupid ass. When you come around my family, respect is expected to be shown and I'ma leave it at that."

"'Ight but know when any of 'em get outta line, it's gonna be straight suck my dick." I shrugged.

"I can't stand your ignorant ass. Let's do what needs to be done, so I can get away from your stupid ass."

"Cool with me. Take ya ass over there to Sea Rise."

"For?"

"Your mark is over that way. You gotta go home with the nigga and-"

"Hold that thought and run it back because I'm sure I heard you wrong."

"Why everything gotta be a fight with you? Do ya ass know how to say okay and then follow up with the action that's being asked of you?"

"Are you forgetting that you said everyone we're going after is connected to Eddy in some way? How do you expect me to have him so interested in me that he takes me back to his place, when I'm sure he knows I'm enemy number 2 right now?"

"How long have you've known Eddy?"

"Since I was 16," she answered.

"Then, you should know that nigga runs on pride. What makes you think he's gonna run his mouth about a female getting one up on him? The only people who know is dude in the room and whoever else is close to him and that's not many. You're good, trust me. I wouldn't put you in harm's way."

"But, you're cool with pimping me out."

"We discussed all of this, so why you bugging now?" I spat. "I never once asked you to fuck any nigga. Whatever you do with ya pussy in the moment is on you."

"Kind of like how you fucked the security guard, right?"

Her tone never changed, but I would be crazy to think there wasn't a bit of jealousy in that.

Chuckling, I said, "I ain't fuck shawty."

"I don't really care if you did or didn't."

"That's why you brought it up, right?"

"I brought it up to make a point."

"Look, let me know mow if you can't play the part because I can find-"

"I can play the part; I just didn't know my survival would weigh so heavily in your hands."

That was bullshit and she knew it. Her whole fucking plan was to have me put a bug in Eddy's ear about leaving her alone.

"Fuck it, don't do it then and, when Eddy comes looking for you, no one can be blamed for the predicament you find yourself in besides you." I shrugged. "I just hope you got some knee pads on standby."

"Nigga, you got me fucked up!" she gritted, then swung her hand.

The slap connected, and I was pissed. I didn't yoke her ass up like I wanted to because if I touched her, my hands weren't gonna be friendly.

"Don't you ever in your raggedy ass life disrespect me like that again. Talking reckless to the right one because I don't have a problem bringing your big headed ass down to size."

"Aye, let that be the last time you put ya hands on me, ight?" I warned.

"James," she spat, putting emphasis on my name. "I'll smack you whenever I feel like it. Keep playing with me and Eddy will be the least of your worries."

Instead of giving her ass the smart remark she was looking for, I gripped her by the wrist and yanked her towards me. I nestled my chin in her neck and whispered, "Keep talking that gangsta shit and I'ma put this pipe in ya life." I brought her right hand to the front of my sweats and ran it along my shaft.

"Eww move!" she squealed, right after she gripped my shit.

"I'm just saying, you're talking my love language right now. I like my bitches nasty and willing to carry a nine," I joked.

"Too bad I have no interest in being your bitch but a nine you can toss my way." She smiled, then leaned up against a tree.

I leaned on the other side and told her who she was looking for. B-Dub was an easy target because he was blinded by pussy. All Keisha had to do was give him some play, let him take her to the crib, then send me a text.

"Please make sure you're on standby. The second I send that text, you need to be on your way."

"Yo, I already told you I got you. What other language you need me to tell you?"

"As if you could. I just wanna make sure we have an understanding."

"When are you gonna put ya trust in me?"

"Not ever!" she laughed.

I moved, so I could look her in the eye and, somehow, I got lost in them. Keisha annoyed the fuck outta me, but I could see myself getting caught up in everything that was her. I was already ready to put the dick in her life and, if the pussy was as fire as she claimed, it was a wrap and her ass was getting knocked up.

Keisha Harper

"Um, you can stop looking at me like that. I'm about to go do this, so be ready."

"Always," he smirked, then lifted my shirt to show me he had it on him. My eyes lingered longer than they should and my mouth watered at the sight of his v cuts. To me, there was nothing sexier than a man's v cuts being hella defined. Jeezy's were so damn crisp that I bit my lip and wondered what it would be like to run my tongue along them, just to get to his dick.

"Who's the one caught up now?"

"It's still you!" I spat.

"Yeah, okay," he laughed.

I shook my headed and went on about my business. My nerves were starting to get the best of me and my hands were starting to sweat. Flirting was my thing, so this should've been an easy task. What had me on edge was the fact I was literally setting a man up to die. He had done nothing wrong to me but because his man's violated, I was put in a position to do the same. I wasn't proud of the things I planned on doing, but I prayed I was forgiven when it came time to be at those pearly gates. To calm myself down, I let my thoughts drift and, of course, they landed on Jeezy. To be around someone other than him was a blessing. He got on my last nerve, but all the bickering we did turned me all the way on. He was a boss and made sure you knew it without having to enforce it. That was sexy as hell to me. Of course, I couldn't let him know that so, for every smart thing he said, I was popping my gums right back.

Walking towards Sea Rise, I nodded my head to some of the dudes that I grew up with. Being in the midst of hood activities wasn't new to me, being on the violent side of it was. Never had I shot a gun and, if I could get past these two weeks without having to, it would be a blessing.

"I know that ain't little Keisha!" someone called out to me.

"Do I know you?" I snapped.

"Damn, so a nigga shared his 62-pack crayons with you and you can't even remember a face. That's crazy," dude laughed.

"I mean, I haven't played with crayons in a minute, so why don't you refresh my memory?"

"Brandon." He smiled.

"Brandon from Mrs. Little's class who had a crush on me?"

"I don't know about that last part but, yeah, that's me."

"What are you doing out here? Last I heard, you got locked up."

"That was a minute ago. I got out a few months back and just been trying to get back right."

"I hear that." I nodded.

Brandon had definitely grew into his looks over the years.

"What you doing over this way?"

"Nothing. Came to see some people, but they weren't around," I answered him.

"Aye B-Dub, we need to hit that lick my nigga. The pussy will be around when you get back," someone said to him.

"B-Dub?"

It came out like a question but it more so a realization. This was who Jeezy wanted me to set up.

"Man, shut the fuck up cause it ain't like that. Give me a minute."

"Don't take all fucking day. You know how that nigga Eddy get."

"Fuck that nigga. His lazy ass don't really want shit no way."

"Be sure to tell him that when he's questioning why we're late," dude said and walked off.

"My bad about that."

"No need to apologize. Duty calls right," I chuckled awkwardly.

I knew this was something we had to do; it just didn't feel right doing it to someone I knew.

"That it does, but let me get your number and we can link up a little later."

"Let me find out you still got that little crush on me."

"Still got, that shit never left. You wasn't trying to give me no play back in the day. I'm trying to see if I can change that."

"Mhm. You can have my number I guess."

"Bet," he smirked, then handed me his phone.

I put my number in and Brandon promised to hit me later in the day. I told him I wasn't gonna hold my breath and walked away. Pulling my phone out, I called Jeezy because something was gonna have to give.

"Yo," he answered.

"Where you at? We need to talk."

"Over by 25th street. Want me to come scoop you?"

"No, I can walk."

"You sure?"

"Yeah, I'll see you in ten," I told him and hung up.

Jeezy was only six blocks away, so the walk wasn't an issue. The real problem was trying to figure out what I was going to do. Setting Brandon up felt wrong, and I was one who took pride in trusting my gut. It could've been the way Brandon talked about Eddy, but it seemed like he would be more valuable alive than dead. Having him on our side would give us the ultimate advantage. Convincing Jeezy of that was going to be the hard part. I was gonna try my hardest to get him to hear me out and follow my lead. If he chose not to, then he would just have to figure handle Brandon on his own.

Finally making it to 25th street, I saw Jeezy chopping it up with some dude. By the time I made it over to where he was, ole boy was walking away and Jeezy was putting his phone away.

"What was that about?"

"Nothing. That's my boy, Casper. He used to run with me."

"What happened?"

"He had other things he wanted to do in his life." Jeezy shrugged.

From the nonchalant tone he gave me, I knew he felt a way about his boy leaving him high and dry.

"That's crazy."

"Right. He still helps me out here and there, but it's not like how it once was."

"Then, why fuck with him?"

"That's family. No matter what, I wouldn't ever turn my back on him. He's the realest nigga I met outside of myself."

"I guess."

"What happened with dude?"

"I know him," I answered, getting straight to it.

"That makes this whole shit ten times easier," he smirked.

"Uh no, it doesn't. It's bad enough I'm setting up dudes I don't know, but I can't do someone I know dirty."

"Keisha-"

He started, but I cut him off, "I already know what you're going to say. Eddy is gunning for us and blah blah blah. I get all that, which is why I came to you with a plan."

"What plan Kesh?"

"While I was talking to him, his boy came over talking about Eddy. Brandon wasn't for the bullshit and how it sounded was like he didn't fuck with him. If we can get Brandon on our team, we can strike from the inside," I explained in one breath.

"How well you know him?"

"We went to elementary together."

"That's the last time you seen the nigga?"

"Yeah. I didn't go to my zone middle and high school."

"You gotta be fucking kidding me," he laughed.

"Did I miss the joke?"

"You are the fucking joke. How are you gonna come to me talking about flipping this nigga to our side and you don't even know dude? For all you know, he could've been baiting your ass. Did you watch his body language when he started talking slick about Eddy? You don't even gotta answer that cause the answer is hell no. You can't just vouch for a nigga because you went to school with him."

"You don't think I know that? I'm not speaking up for him on a whim. I know what I felt in my gut and I'm telling you this is the right move."

"My life and livelihood is on the line. I'm not bout to put it in the hands of your gut. Shit is going down how we planned."

"Then, you're doing it solo because I want no parts."

"I don't have a problem with doing it dolo, but know the extra blood that's gonna flow is on your hands."

"You can't blame me for that."

"Yes, the fuck I can. You're the one stepping out and, without you, that nigga is gonna be with his people and ain't no survives when I'm spraying."

"How can you talk about trust and me having faith in you, when you can't even trust me? I would never intentionally bring harm your way. All I'm doing is trusting that there's a different way to handle this. So, why can't you trust me and let me play the lead?"

"This shit gonna come back and bite me in the ass, but you got it. You meet up with the nigga and swag him to this side. Whatever happens after that falls on you."

"I'll handle the consequences," I assured him.

"You don't gotta choice."

He gave me one last look before jumping in the car. I followed his lead and got in, then started wondering what I was going to say to Brandon. Too much was weighing on this one conversation, so I had to get it right because I didn't want to see what happened if I got it wrong.

* * *

"Game time," I whispered to myself as Jeezy dropped me off up the block from Brandon's spot. An hour or so before seven, he hit my phone asking if I wanted to roll through. I played hard to get before giving in. I had Jeezy drive me, just in case I need him to stand in.

"Wassup beautiful," Brandon greeted.

"Hey." I smiled

It took about ten minutes to get down the block and up to his place. I looked around and it was nice. I guess not having a lot of furniture in the crib was a guy thing.

Brandon's place wasn't as empty as Jeezy's but it didn't have everything it could've.

"You wanna sit down while I get the wine?"

"Oh, you got wine for me?"

"I'll get whatever for you if it means I can have you in my presence," he flirted.

"You're laying it on kind of thick."

"I gotta. I know you got dudes lining up around the block trying to get at you. I've heard about you, Ms. Keisha."

"All good things I hope."

"Something like that," he answered, then passed me my glass.

"But, wassup with you? What you been into?"

"Nothing really. I sell a little weed here and there but nothing major. I actually get my stuff from Eddy. You know him, don't you?"

"Can't be the same Eddy I'm hustling for."

"He be out there in Bedstuy?"

"Yeah. That's crazy. How you hook up with him?"

"Long story. Wassup with the two of you? It seemed like y'all had issues earlier."

"We got our little tiffs but it's nothing I can't handle."

"What if I said he could be a thing of our past?"

I threw that out there because beating around the bush wasn't working. I needed to get out what I wanted to say, so I could get back to my regular life.

"You shouldn't speak that type of energy into the atmosphere Kesh," he warned.

"I know, but he's not who you think he is. He beat me crazy because of some foul shit that he did."

"And he's gonna get what's coming to him for that."

"That's what I'm trying to put you on to. Me and-"

I was talking so fast and trying to get my point across that I never saw it coming. If it wasn't for the sound of the gun being cocked back, my ass would've still been running off at the mouth.

"Wha... what are you doing Brandon?"

"Come on Kesh, you should know better than that. You came up in my crib talking shit about boss man. You think I'ma just let it ride that you're trying to take him out?"

"I thought you-"

"Ya ass thought wrong. That nigga Jeezy should've taught you better than that. You made this shit too easy. Eddy said all I had to do was talk the right shit and you would take the bait. I just ain't think you would slip up so fast."

"You don't have to do this Brandon."

"I don't, but I'ma pull this trigger, then go and collect my money."

At this point, there was nothing more I could've said. Niggas were so hard up for money, they would do anything if it meant getting a bag. My dumb ass should've listened to Jeezy but, because I was letting my emotions lead the way, I fucked up. I was out here playing a dangerous game and allowing my feelings guide me. At this point, I deserved to die because I brought this on myself. It was my consequence and probably my fate. I closed my eyes, waiting for the bullets to tear through my flesh.

A single gunshot went off and I swear it was taking forever to enter my body.

"Open ya fucking eyes stupid!" Jeezy barked.

"Wha... what happened?"

I opened my eyes and Brandon's body laid there lifeless.

"I saved ya life, that's what happened. What did you touch in here?"

"Just the wine."

"Stay here," he told me, then dashed towards the back of the house.

A few minutes later, he came running back towards the front with a duffle bag and yelling that we had to leave now. I rushed out the front door making sure I snatched the wine glass. We walked out of the building as if we lived there and jumped in his car. Jeezy pulled off not saying a word, but it wasn't like he had to. I already knew I fucked up, just like I knew he was gonna let my ass have it.

James 'Jeezy' Brown

"**T**ake this duffle bag upstairs with you. Drop it in my room," I instructed Keisha.

Besides the few words I just said to her, I ain't have nothing for her. The bullshit she pulled showed just how naive and green she was to all of this. She loved popping shit like she was bout it bout it when, in reality, her heart was pure as the day she was born. For the type of job I was using her for, that heart of hers was gonna get the both of us killed. The way I saw it, I needed to cut her ass loose. Couldn't have her jeopardizing all that I had going on and what kind of nigga would I be if I changed who she was for my own personal gain?

"You're not coming upstairs?" she questioned with sad eyes.

"Nah."

"I know you're upset with me, but I think we need to talk about this."

"Go upstairs. I'll be back in a few."

She gazed at me before she stepped out the car with an attitude.

"Aye, don't be slamming my shit," I told her.

"Kiss my ass!" she spat back.

She headed inside, and I pulled off with a million and one things on my mind. When shit got like this for me, there was only one person I could chop it up with. I sent a text letting 'em know I was on my way. After that, I turned my shit off and enjoyed the silence of the drive. An hour or so later, I pulled up to Issa's crib.

"Jeezy, what are you doing here?" Issa asked, opening the door.

"You ain't get my text?"

"Obviously not if I'm asking what you're doing here."

I tried to walk in her apartment and she held her hand out, stopping me. "You got company?"

"If I did, it wouldn't be your business."

"Yeah ight, move."

"What are we doing Jeezy?"

"I'm trying to come in and have a conversation with you, but you acting brand new."

"There's nothing new about how I'm acting. But, I can't be that person for you, anymore. I love you, Jeezy, and you know that but-"

"Sayless Issa," I told her, not beat for the bullshit.

"No, you need to hear this. I love you, Jeezy, and my heart yearns for you. Putting you on hold the way I did to focus on school was wrong, but it's what I needed to do for me. Making sure I'm straight is more important to me than a future with you."

"Damn," I mumbled.

"I know it sounds harsh, but it's the truth. After how you treated me the last time we were together, I took some time to think and assess the situation."

"And what you figure out?"

"That I gotta let you go. I got jealous when I heard you talking to a female so much that I was willing to put my studying on hold just to keep you with me. That's toxic and I don't want to be that. I want you to be happy, especially without me. I know what I mean to you and-"

"Meant," I corrected.

"Excuse me?"

"You know what you meant to me... past tense. All this shit you're talking is pointless. I haven't gave a fuck about you since we were jits. The life I was trying to give you isn't for you anymore. You weren't shit but pussy to me these last couple of years," I explained harshly. "That little speech you're giving is cute, but I don't give a fuck so you can hold that."

"Woooowwww!" she sang and started clapping. "You know if I didn't know you so well, I would've took that to heart. You can act like I mean nothing, but we both know better. Like I told you before, I'm the end and the beginning; it's only a matter of if I want to step up and play that role. Whatever bitch got you feeling yourself will never amount to me. Remember that the next time you feel it's cool to call me just a fuck!"

She slammed the door in my face like I was nothing. I chuckled softly, then left out and jumped back in my car. A nigga was burnt out and being around Keisha wasn't the move. I was a mark in these streets but, with the way I was feeling, it ain't mean shit to me. I was in need of some green, liquor, and pussy and, if death was gonna greet me at the door, so fucking be it.

* * *

Stumbling into the crib, I locked the door behind me, went straight to my weed stash and made sure my duffle was in the room.

"Umm, we getting lit in here or in the living room?"

"Go chill in the living room," I told my pussy for the night.

She walked away, and I knocked on the guest room door. Keisha opened it dressed in a sports bra and some shorts. My eyes roamed her body until she cleared her throat, fucking up my train of thought.

"How can I help you?" I smirked.

"You came and knocked on this door," she sassed. Squinting at me, she asked, "Are you okay?"

"I'm good. I knocked on ya door to let you know I have company. You don't gotta stay in ya room but, if you ain't trying to get piped down, ain't no point in coming out."

"Company? Who do you have here with you, Jeezy?"

"I already told you, company!"

"And I'm asking who the hell is company!"

"That ain't your concern, just think about what I said bout fucking," I chuckled and walked away.

"What you find in there to drink?" I questioned ole girl.

"You had some wine but nothing harder. I'ma need some Cîroc vanilla if we gonna get right."

"Shit, liquor store two block up."

"It's three in the morning. I'm not going out there alone," she complained.

"Then, ya ass don't want no Cîroc," I laughed.

"Then, I guess ya ass don't want no pussy."

"Aye listen, I already got the top, so I'm cool on everything else. Fucking was more for your benefit than mine."

"Nigga, you got me-"

"Jeezy, who the fuck is this and why is my wine bottle in her hand?" Keisha barked.

She stood at the end of the hallway with her hip poked out and her arms folded across her chest.

"I already told you I had company."

"Keyword being *you* have company. Her being your peoples mean she shouldn't be touching my stuff."

"Sweetheart, if this is your lightweight shit, I'm sorry. I was just trying to catch a buzz before fucking his fine ass."

"If you need a buzz to fuck, then maybe you shouldn't be fucking," Keisha spat. "Jeezy, can I talk to you?"

"Words are coming outta ya mouth, ain't they?"

"I wanna talk in private."

"You can say what you need to in front of Lexi."

"Samantha," she corrected.

"Doesn't matter, the pussy and mouth are both nameless."

"Okayyy," Keisha sang, walking towards Samantha. She snatched her wine outta her hand then said, "It's time for you to dip."

"I'm not going anywhere. I came here to get some dick, so that's what I'ma get."

"How about I toss ya ass a banana and a condom?"

"Funny but I don't do fake dick."

"You might wanna look into it because this dick," Keisha smacked, "isn't sliding in any of the holes you have to offer."

"Oh baby, you're a little too late. One of my holes already had the pleasure of the dick," Samantha snickered. "Jeezy, call me when your groupie learns to dismiss herself."

"Groupie!"

Man, that was the last word to be heard before Keisha started beating the black off ole girl. Too fucked up to deal with the bullshit, I grabbed the wine and my weed, then went straight for my bedroom.

Keisha

Heated wasn't even close to how I was feeling right now. I was seeing nothing but red as I paced back and forth. I didn't know what had gotten into Jeezy, but he was dead wrong for bringing that bitch over here. If he wanted to fuck, he should've took her to a motel where her hoe ass belonged. Then, to add salt to the injury, he left us in the living room tussling. I mean, I beat ole girl's ass and dragged her right out the door, but it was the principle of the whole thing. As soon as she got out of line, Jeezy should've checked her. I started to bust in his room and let his stupid ass have it, but I wanted to get my thoughts together. Whatever I said to him, I needed it to ring off. I needed for him to know he was playing around with the wrong bitch. I gave myself a cool twenty minutes before I headed down the hallway. Knocking on the door was out of the question because privacy and being polite was out of the window.

"You know you have a lot of fucking nerve bringing that bitch up in here. Since I've met you, you're dumb ass been talking about trusting you and putting my faith in you. How am I supposed to do any of that when you'll allow some random to disrespect me, all because she's willing to give up the pussy?!"

My mouth was running so fast, I didn't even notice the gloomy expression on his face until I heard faint sobs.

"Nigga, are you crying?" I questioned, twisting up my face.

"Go to ya room ight," he said, never looking my way.

I stood there wondering what I was supposed to do in this moment. I'd never been around a nigga while he was having a sentimental moment. A part of me wanted to tell him to suck it the fuck up because nothing he was going through was as bad as he was making it. I nixed that idea because it was toxic as fuck. Then, I wanted to continue on with my rant, but the better half of my heart felt bad and wanted to know what was wrong.

"You wanna talk about it?"

"Nah."

"Fine, fuck it then," I spat and started to head out of his room.

I only made it halfway out the door before I turned around, slammed the door behind me and got all in his face.

"You're sitting in this bitch with a bottle of wine and tears in your eyes, if that's not a cry for a listening ear, then I don't know what is. I usually don't do this but, for the sake of knowing how it feels to need someone and no one be there, I'll be that listening ear. What I'm not going to do is beg you to talk to me, but I will say this. Don't let the street in you be the reason you continue to hurt inside."

Jeezy not only didn't say anything, but he still didn't bother to look my way. I was all up in his face, yet his eyes stayed a good distance from mine.

"Whatever then," I mumbled and got up.

My fingers had just gripped the door knob when I heard his lighter flick and his raspy voice call out to me.

"Yeah," I answered.

"I'm not even trying to be on no tough guy shit. Speaking on feelings isn't something that most females are cool with. Shit, half of 'em don't give a fuck no way. All they want is to fuck and for a nigga to throw money their way."

"Good thing I'm not any of them bitches. I know we have our differences and we're both scared of letting go, but something heavy is on your mind. My life is on the line and, if we're going to save it, I need you to be a hundred percent in the game."

"You ever been in love?" he asked randomly, then hit his blunt.

"Um, what you mean like kiddie high school love? Only one nigga was able to pull me in high school and I don't think I was in love but, shit, I was in like heavy," I laughed.

"Nah, that's not what I'm talking about. I mean real love, that shit that'll make you lay your life on the line for the other person. Have you agreeing to stupid ass terms, just so you can have that person in ya life."

"You mean the type of love that'll have you out here looking a fool. Nope, I've never been in that type of love and I don't want to be. Seems toxic as fuck."

"I wouldn't call it toxic, but that shit fucks with ya head."

"You've been in love like that with someone?"

"Mannnn," he chuckled, then passed me the blunt.

I moved over to the bed, took it from him, and sat down, eagerly waiting to hear the story.

"I don't even know where to start other than Issa could've got whatever she wanted from me. She was the type of chick you kill for and then turn around and do the time for the kill. She was it for me. I had life planned out and I swear I was gon' make all her dreams come true."

"What happened? You cheated?"

"Fuck outta here, cheating never crossed my mind."

"Then, what happened? When a nigga feels that strongly about a female, it's rare he lets her go, even if she doesn't want to be with him."

"That's facts, but I ain't let her go as easily as it might seem. She wanted to focus on school, and I respected that. Our relationship became nothing but dick and pussy appointments. After a while, I saw what it was and feelings started to fade. I still fucked cause the pussy was good, but the attachment wasn't there."

"I don't believe that you kept her around because you wanted to fuck. You could've found any bitch to fuck on. There was something more keeping you there."

"Other than the pussy, nah."

"Bullshit."

"I'm deadass."

"Who was the person you could be vulnerable with?"

"Her."

"Even after y'all stopped dating?"

"Shit, I guess."

"That right there is the reason you kept her on call. She was the outlet you didn't know you needed."

"Maybe but that shit is over and down with now."

"I hope I don't have anything to do with it."

"Don't flatter yaself," he laughed. "She got a big head about the whole situation. Issa think she got me on the back burner and she can fuck with me whenever."

"I mean, isn't that how you niggas think?"

"That's different."

"It's only different because you're the one being played like a bitch."

"Watch ya mouth," he warned.

"I didn't mean any disrespect, but I'm just saying. You dudes love having the chick that you really want to be with standing on the sideline while all the hoes are in the game. Now, it's flipped and you can't stand the heat."

"You don't even understand the game but love to spit it."

"Oh, I understand it; you just don't want to admit it."

"Ain't shit to admit. We keep our future on the sideline, so she don't gotta go through all the hardships. Females love to say they'll hold a nigga down but, when the time comes, they end up wearing their hearts on their sleeves. I've seen some of my niggas be talking to a female and their lady walk right up and slap ole girl. The conversation wasn't even nothing outta line but, because she feels a way, shit gotta get violence. No dude wants to deal with that and they don't wanna see their lady go through it."

"I mean, he should know his girl is crazy and doesn't want him in other females' faces conversing."

"It can't be like that though. That's where trust and loyalty come in, but no female is truly ready to have that conversation."

"I am."

"Ya ass can't even listen to the game I be kicking, so I know for sure you ain't ready to talk trust and loyalty."

"What game have you been trying to kick?"

"I told you that shit with ole boy wasn't going to work out?"

"That isn't game and I didn't listen because up until I heard you sobbing, I didn't think you had any feelings."

"I wasn't sobbing. A tear or two fell off the strength of who I thought my wife would be talking real greasy when I was trying to talk to her about real life shit."

"If that's what you wanna call it, I'm not going to judge." I shrugged. "I know you didn't go to her with our Eddy problem?"

"She's the voice of reasoning when I'm ready to go off the deep end," he said nonchalantly.

"Okay, but she knows nothing about me and I don't need her knowing my business. You could've came to me if you needed to be talked off the ledge. This shit we got going on is between me and you."

"Nah, this shit we got going on is real fucking personal when it come to me. I'm not out here bodying niggas for the hell of it; I'm fighting for my livelihood. I have two other people I gotta take care of and I don't have time to fucking waste. That stunt you pulled could've ended ya life and fucked up my plans."

"You might be fighting for you livelihood, but I'm fighting for my fucking life!" I spat.

I felt the need to defend myself because Jeezy had me feeling like I was just out here fucking up because I wanted to. I made an honest mistake and he needed to understand that.

"I'm sorry that I can't be a stone cold killer like you."

"It's not even about that. I've never put a gun in ya hand and I'll be damn if I asked you to pull the trigger. All I need from you is to have conversation with these dudes. Once I get in the door, you can dip and I'll handle the rest. You'll never have to know what happened or how it went down but, when you make mistakes, you get yourself involved in things you need to know nothing about."

"So, where do we go from here?"

"Shit, I don't know. I'm ready to just run up on this nigga Eddy and body any nigga that tries to come after me because of it."

"That's not smart, especially when you left Brandon's body to be found."

"Why you think I'm still at the crib?" he smirked.

"Whatever." I rolled my eyes.

"Real shit Kesh. If you can't stomach what we're doing, then you need to walk away now. You won't have to worry about Eddy; I'll make sure nothing happens to you."

"How can I trust that?"

"How many more times do I have to save you for you to see you can trust a nigga? I don't wanna see you hurt and I put that on everything."

"But, why?"

We locked eyes; then, he moved as close to me as he could get. He cupped my chin and said, "Cause I need you on the sidelines while I play in the game with the hoes."

"Get the hell outta my face with that dumb shit," I spat, pushing him away.

"Ease up cause you know that was funny."

101

"Not funnier than ya big ass crying," I joked.

"I bet I can make you cry."

"Give it your best shot," I challenged.

"Get naked," he smirked.

"What?"

"You heard me."

"Boy, bye. I'm not even into all of that and I'm damn sure not into you."

"That's bullshit, but I'ma let you have it."

"No, it's facts."

"I'm going to bed. Make sure you don't invite any other weak hoes over here," I told him.

"Make sure you think about what I said. This ya last chance to bow out gracefully!" he called after me.

I nodded my head but didn't have a clue what I was going to do.

James 'Jeezy' Brown

Waking up the next morning, a nigga's head was bussing. That liquor had got the best of the kid and I was paying for that shit. I eased out of bed and headed for the kitchen to get something to drink. My mouth was dry like a muthafucker and my stomach was growling like crazy. I was all fucked up and was wishing Samantha's ass would've been around to get me right.

"Good morning!" Keisha greeted, sounding real cheery.

"Wassup, you good?" I asked, looking at her strangely.

"I'm fine, and why are you looking at me like that?"

"Cause I been around you for a week and some days and ya ass ain't never wake up cooking and sounding happy to see me."

"Okayy," she said awkwardly.

"Cut the bullshit and tell me wassup." My head was hurting too much to be playing mind games with Kesha.

"We can talk while we eat. Take a seat."

"Nah Kesh, just tell me what's going on. My head booming and shit."

"Drink this."

She passed me some green type of drink that smelled straight like ass.

"Fuck is this?"

"The answer to that hangover you got. Drink it and shut up."

"Aye, you talking real greasy. What the fuck happened last night for you to switch up on me?"

"Oh, you don't remember?"

"I was fucked up like a muthafucker. All I remember is leaving the spot with Samantha and ya two getting into a fight. After that, shit is a blur."

"How can you remember the fight but nothing else?"

"Cause when I went in my room, I threw back wine and some henny I had stashed."

"You were really trying to forget some things, huh?"

"Something like that."

I took a sip of the drink and almost knocked Keisha's head off for giving me this shit. It tasted worse than it smelled and wasn't no way I was finishing it.

"To make a long story short, you opened up to me and I really appreciate that. I figure the least I can do is cook you breakfast since I'm not gonna be opening up no time soon," she giggled.

"Damn, I thought we were making progress."

"Some things take a lifetime to bury and others take more than a week and some days to reveal."

"That's deep."

"Yeah, well, I'ma deep person when I'm not being snappy."

"I can fuck with it," I smirked, then took the time to admire her.

The Keisha in front of me wasn't the Kesh that was popping shit all the time. She was relaxed and chilled. Her natural beauty was amplified by her calm demeanor, and I was really fucking with it.

"Don't go falling in love because I don't play the sideline."

"Chill, I would never; you would be in the game by my side."

"Uh huh, tell me anything," she giggled.

"What you cook?"

"Nothing special. Spinach and cheese omelet and home fries."

"Sounds good."

I took my seat at the table after dumping out the rest of that nasty ass drink. Keisha sat my plate down and sat across from me. We ate quietly, only speaking when something needed to be passed to the other.

"Damn," I sighed, pushing back from the table.

"I did my thing, huh?"

"It was ight," I joked. "I've had better."

"Bullshit. You can't never give a girl her props."

"I give 'em when they're deserved."

"Whatever. We need to talk about this whole Eddy thing."

Just like that, shit got serious real quick.

"Wassup?"

"Last night you asked me did I wanna step because this was the last chance I was going to get. I stayed up all night thinking about it."

"Ight, what you decide?"

"I can't do it. I might pop off a lot and you know talking shit is a second language to me, but I'm not about that murder life, no matter how much I may want to be."

"How you say that but got into this whole mess because you snipping off dicks?" I asked, confused by what she was saying. "I don't even see why you're tripping; you're not the one killing."

"I'm not, but I'm still involved. It's the beginning of summer and I'm spending mine trying to set niggas up that did nothing to me. That's wild," she explained, shaking her head.

"Yo, you got into this by being on some gangsta shit and, now, you wanna just chill and catch the summer vibes. Fuck you mean?" I spat. "This type a shit all the vibes you gon' catch during a summer in Brooklyn. This shit ain't out of the ordinary."

"Just hear me out."

"Keisha-"

"Just hear me out James, damn!" she spat.

"Ight, you got it, speak."

"By no means am I saying I didn't bring this on myself. I cut that nigga's dick because he *deserved* it. These men you want me to set up didn't do a thing to me. All I'm saying is let's leave them alone and focus on Eddy. It's a known fact in war that when you dismantle the head, the body is going to fall. All you have to do is take him out and everyone else will fall in line."

"And what if they don't?"

"What's the odds of them not? From how you talk about how niggas flipped on you, loyalty isn't law for these dudes. All they care about is getting money. As long as you give them a way to get it, they gonna go for it."

"You just got it all figured out, huh?"

"You ain't even hear the half."

"Let me know lil baby."

Keisha's ass wasn't lying when she said she been up all night thinking. The plan she laid out for me was damn near flawless. The setup wasn't too different from how we were gonna play all these other niggas. Instead of it being one chick getting at Eddy, it was going to be two. Keisha wanted to use her cousins to lure Eddy to an apartment. From there, Keisha and I would handle things. The plan wasn't bad and it probably could work, but putting my faith in fake loyalty wasn't gonna fly. I learned my lesson the first time bout that shit. Whoever got down with me was gonna have to be dudes I could trust.

"So, what you think?"

"I'll let you know."

"Wait, what? The plan is bulletproof."

"It's cool. Thanks for breakfast," I told her and kissed her cheek.

I went back in my room, grabbed my phone and sent Casper a text, letting him know we needed to get up. Despite him doing his own thing, Casper was the only nigga I trusted enough to take advice from.

* * *

"Where the fuck you been at?" Casper greeted when I stepped out the car.

"Staying low and trying to get back right."

"I already told you I got some shit lined up for you. Just say the word."

"I 'preciate that, but what you have going on isn't for me. The gun thing you do is cool, but the club shit doesn't peek my interest. I like the thrill of this street shit, feel me?"

"The thrill doesn't last long, my nigga. We got into this shit at what, sixteen? We were getting out of school and making plays for the big dawgs. Then, we became the big dawgs and shit was cool. I got what I needed to get and dipped."

"And that's cool... for you."

"It should've been cool for you. We fucking twenty-five and ya ass is still trying to be it. This shit long term. At what point is enough enough?"

"Fuck if I know. You the one who had a change of heart. Why don't you tell me?"

"Things changed for me when I had my daughter. I wasn't just out here living for myself."

"I ain't got shit to live for except myself." I shrugged.

108

My family meant the world to me, but hustling was providing them with the funds to live the life they deserved to live. If this street shit took me out, I knew Casper would make sure my people were straight.

"You gotta change that shit and settle down. Get you a thoroughbred and have some babies," he laughed.

"Man, these women don't know shit about loyalty. What I look like making one of them my baby moms? I'm good on all that shit."

"Ight. I'm not bout to preach ya head off. Wassup, what was so urgent?"

"Remember how I told you I had a solution for my Eddy problem?"

"Yeah, I thought he would've been handled by now. Word is he's on ya head. One of his boys out in Sea Rise got popped."

"His day is coming, just not as fast as I would've liked."

"What happened?"

"For me to get this down, I would have to compromise someone else's character and I'm not really trying to do that."

"Since when you give a fuck about anyone else?"

"I don't. Shawty just different and I don't-"

"Oh, this about a chick," he laughed. "For someone who don't have nothing to live for, you damn sure taking ole girl feelings into consideration."

"She been through some shit and I'm not tryna drag her through more."

"Ight, so what's the alternative?"

I ran down the plan to him that Keisha came up with and, just like her, he thought the plan was solid.

"That shit not a bad plan. You get the shit done sooner than you wanted and ole girl will be straight. If you play it right, ya money could be back where it used to be in a month and the rest of the summer could be spent getting to know shawty better."

"We ain't rocking like that. She just cool. Her ass gonna be my best friend or some shit."

"Bullshit!" he laughed. "Run with her plan and handle that. If you need me, hit my line and I'll come outta retirement quick."

"I got this bruh," I told him.

We talked for a little while before I took off. I didn't head straight back to the crib because I wanted to do something nice for Keisha. I'd been beating her head in about trusting me and shit but never gave her a real reason too. Words weren't going to gain her trust, so I had to show action.

Keisha

"I just don't understand how you can be around him for all this time and not get into something," Bailey smacked in the phone. "Jeezy fine as fuck and, if you don't hurry up, I'ma offer him all of his punanni."

"Do you have to be such a hoe?" Kylie asked.

"What you call a hoe, I say is liberating. Why can men sling their dick every which way, but I have to be stingy with the kitty. Shit, Sire is out here fucking like it's a marathon when he already had the prize at home. If that nigga wanna be funny, then I'ma be fucking hilarious. So, let Jeezy know I'm interested in seeing what the dick do," she laughed.

"Maybe Sire would take ya ass seriously if you stopped treating your vagina like a revolving door!" I gritted, annoyed.

Bailey talking about Jeezy the way she was shouldn't have bothered me because he wasn't mine. He was for the streets, but I'd be lying if I said a part of me didn't want him to be for me.

"And just like that, we've uncovered this hoe's feelings for him."

"Shut up Bailey because Keisha's not feeing his sneaky ass," Kylie defended.

"Both of y'all hoes are in denial. She likes him, don't you, Kesh?"

"I meannnnnn…" I dragged out my words to avoid admitting the truth.

"Keisha!!" Kylie shouted. "That nigga is foul as fuck and you need to leave his ass alone."

"How do you know he's foul?" I asked.

"The streets talk and I've been listening."

"Just because they talk doesn't mean the truth is always being told."

"Yeah, ya ass like him. Look at how you're capping for the nigga."

"It's not even like that," I sighed, trying to save face.

"If you like him, then so be it. All I'ma say is this; you need to watch that nigga and the way he moves."

"I appreciate the concern, but I'm fine. I'll text y'all later okay," I told them, no longer wanting to talk. I originally called them to run my idea by them about the Eddy situation. Before I could even get it out, Bailey was jumping down my throat about what I had going on with Jeezy.

"Mhmm. Bye," Kylie sassed.

"Don't pay her ignorant ass no mind. You know how she is when it comes to you. Love you, cuz," Bailey sang and hung up.

I tossed my phone to the left of me and laid back, just to stare up at the ceiling. Out of everyone in my life, Kylie was probably the person I was the closest too. Bailey was my baby, but she was too much all of the time. Phour thought I was ratchet and ghetto, when I had nothing on Bailey. Kylie was just like me in so many ways that it scared me. We were both just trying to figure out life all the while having fun and doing what we wanted. We marched to our own beats and always stood up for what we believed in. That's why I couldn't understand why she was acting so funky towards Jeezy and how I might've felt about him. She knew better than anyone that allowing a man into my personal space wasn't something I did often. I flirted with my fair share of men and fucked more than a few, but none of them could ever say they knew me on a personal level. I was guarded and I planned on remaining that way until someone came along and showed me that it was okay to be different. So far, Jeezy had been the only dude to attempt to do that.

He showed interest in getting to know me without being on my body heavy. Any other dude would've been pressed to sex if I was staying with them. Other than Jeezy bringing that bitch over here, he'd been nothing but respectful. Even him yoking me up didn't bother me because that's what a nigga was going to do when provoked. As long as he didn't lay hands on me, we would be cool. I honestly couldn't really explain what I felt for Jeezy. It wasn't like I was interested in being with him, but I felt an urge to protect me. I didn't want to see him dead the same way he didn't want to see me hurt. All of it was confusing and all I could do was hope that when all of this was over, I would gain some clarity on my feelings or lack thereof.

"Aye Kesh, you up?" I heard Jeezy call out to me.

I jumped out of bed because I never heard him walk through the front door. Meeting him in the living room, I almost gasped. He was standing there with a few sunflowers in hand, along with Chinese food from my favorite spot. The gesture was cute; I just didn't know how to take it because when he left earlier, he seemed upset.

"What's all of this?" I asked.

"What it look like?" he shot cockily.

"Do you always gotta be an ass? Just answer the question because I don't want to assume."

"It's me doing something nice for you."

"Why?"

113

"Why what?"

"Why are you doing something nice for me? Like, what does this mean?" My voice was caught all in my throat, making my tone sound childlike and unsure.

"I wanted to ease some of the tension this situation been putting on you. What we got going on could break the hardest bitch. You're not even close to being hard and you're standing true. I appreciate that shit and just wanted to show it."

"So, those are for me?" I quizzed, putting to the flowers.

"Who else they gonna be for? Ya big headed ass is probably the only chick on earth that has a thing for sunflowers."

"Shut up!" I giggled, then took them from his hands to smell. "These are my favorite; how did you know?"

"It's not hard to tell. You have a big ass sunflower on ya thigh and another one with a quote on your collarbone."

"Oh, so you've been watching my body," I smirked and took the food from his hand.

"Not at all, a nigga pays attention to detail," he laughed, then followed me into the kitchen.

I grabbed us some plates and grabbed the bottle of wine I picked up from the liquor store while he was out. Pouring us some of the wine, I said, "Is that not studying my body?"

"I see I'ma have to break it down for you. Studying your body would be me outlining ya frame with the tips of my fingers, then retracing those lines with the tip of my tongue. If I was to study your body, I would eat ya pussy until I could describe in detail what it taste like and how your pearl throbs when you're nearing an orgasm," he explained.

"I... uh... I..."

"You don't gotta say shit lil baby. Just know when I study ya body, you'll be calling a nigga daddy."

"Whatever," I sassed, rolling my eyes.

I picked up one of the cartons and started piling food on my plate. Everything Jeezy said had me so off balance. A few times I missed my plate all together and the food went falling on the table. I felt stupid, but Lord knows I wanted to feel his words just as deeply as I heard them. This was the second time he talked about his sex game and, I swear the more he talked about it, the more I wanted to throw the pussy his way.

"I thought about the idea you kicked earlier."

"Oh yeah?"

"Yeah," he laughed.

"What's so funny?"

"That shit I said fucked ya head up huh?"

"Not even," I lied.

"Yeah ight. Ya ass still thinking bout that shit. What you wanna do Kesh? You wanna lay ya lips on top of mine?"

"No one wants to kiss your ugly ass," I sassed.

"You got the wrong lips in mind lil baby," he smirked.

"So damn nasty! Can you just tell me what you think about the plan please?" I told him, refusing to look at him.

"Look at me," he demanded.

"I'm good, just talk."

"You gotta look at me if you want me to speak. That shy shit don't fly over here, especially when I know ya ass got mouth for days."

Slowly bringing my eyes up to his, I tried my best not to get caught up.

"Happy? What did you decide?"

"I'll be happier if I was blowing ya back out, but that's a different conversation for another day," he laughed. "As far as your plan goes, we can fuck with it, on one condition tho."

"What?"

"When it's all said and done, you gotta kick it with me."

"Kick it how?"

"Real shit, I don't know. All I know is I want you around. Give me ya time and I'll give you mine."

"Giggling, I replied, "Let me find out you want me in ya world."

"I want more than that but, for now, I'll settle for kicking it with you."

"I might be able to handle that, as long as you don't have me out here looking a fool. I don't play that bench shit and I refuse to watch another bitch be in the game with ya ass. If you want my time, then my time is the only time your ass better be able to afford."

"Damn, we starting off like that? I ain't say I wanted to fuck; I just wanna spend time."

"Oh, so talking about eating my pussy isn't you wanting to fuck?"

"Nah, lil baby, that's me wanting to sample before I make a commit."

"You got me all the way fucked up. The only way to sample is to commit," I smirked.

"Fuck it then, you'll just miss out on the best orgasm of ya life."

"Don't write a check those pretty lips can't cash," I told him, smiling.

"I can put my lips where my money is. The real question is are you up for it?"

"I have a better idea in mind, let's play truth or dear. If we don't wanna do the dare, then we throw back two shots. If we don't wanna tell the truth, then you gotta knock down three. You game?"

"I'll fuck with it, but I'm not playing with wine. We got some brown or something."

"I got us covered. Just be ready because I don't play fair; I play to win."

"Man, come in the living room with the shit," he said, then got up from the table.

I went into the guest room and grabbed the bottle of D'usse I brought early. From there, I went in the living room and sat on the floor Indian-style.

"Oh, we slumming it?"

"What, you too good to drink out the bottle and sit on the floor? You don't have cooties or anything, right?"

"We good baby."

"Cool. You wanna go first?"

"Nah, you got it, do ya thing."

"Truth. I'll play in to ya hand."

I sat and thought of something to ask. I didn't want to dare him because I wanted to learn more about him. My interest in him was purely off how he moved and the way he handled me. I didn't know much about him, besides that he was a hustling muthafucker and was big on loyalty and trust. I wanted to dig deeper and wasn't a better way than to ask those hard questions while liquor was in the system.

"I'ma start off light. Did you fuck that security guard to get the tape?"

"You still tripping on that shit?"

"I'm not tripping, I just want to know, so are you gonna answer or take them shots?"

"Pass that bottle. I'ma take them shots."

"What?" I spat, annoyed.

"We gotta explain why we don't want to answer?" he chuckled.

"No but you could've answered that question. It's a yes or no."

"And now it's a you'll never know."

"Here." I passed him the bottle and rolled my eyes hella hard.

There was no reason other than he wanted to fuck with me for him not to answer that question. For whatever reason, I felt some type of way about the situation and wanted to know the truth.

"Ight, my turn. Truth or dare?"

"Dare."

"Ight, I see you, big Kesh. I dare you to strip down to ya bra and panties."

"You would say some freak shit like that."

"I love to admire a work of art."

"Admire all you want because you'll never touch this canvas."

I stood up and stripped out of my sweats and crop top. Just to fuck with him, I did a cute little spin and made both of my ass cheeks jump.

"Keep playing with me and I'ma have ya ass lovesick Keisha. I'm trying to spare you from that shit, but you keep trying me."

"Whatever. Truth or dare."

"Dare."

"Strip."

"That's nothing."

"Ass naked," I smirked.

"Done! I don't like chilling in clothes anyway."

He took all his stuff off, then threw his briefs my way before sitting back down. I couldn't even go off on his ass for doing that nasty shit because my eyes were fixated on his dick. It was the prettiest dick I'd ever seen in my life. Hairless, thick, veins popping, and so damn chocolatey.

"Damn, we would make some pretty chocolate babies," I mumbled unconsciously.

"You tryna give a nigga kids just from seeing the dick?" he laughed.

"Huh, what?"

"I heard that shit you said, but I'ma let you live. Truth or Dare?"

"Truth."

"What happened to make you become so guarded?"

Soon as that question left his lips, I snatched the bottle up and took my shots. Wasn't no way I was telling that story.

James 'Jeezy' Brown

Keisha thought she was fooling someone with this truth or dare bullshit, but I saw right through it. Her whole persona came off as this tough chick who didn't need a soul and didn't take shit from no one. She might've fooled some people with that shit, but I saw the real her. The her that she was too afraid to show because of past hurt. Messing with Keisha was gon' be a marathon and I didn't know if I was up for it in the long haul but, for the moment, I was all in. Her mean ass had a nigga ready to guard her heart with all I had and dead anyone who caused her pain. She had me fucked up in the head and, the more time we spent together, the worse it was going to get.

"Ight, if I'ma sit here naked, this shit gotta get popping. Come harder or don't come at all," I told her after she put the bottle down.

"Fine, truth or dare?"

"Fuck it, truth."

"Do you think you'll ever be in love again after the stuff your ex put you through?"

"Pass that bottle lil baby."

"Damn, I didn't take you to be pussy," she giggled.

"Run that back."

"I mean, you picked truth before and took shots, then you pick it again, just to take more shots. What's the point in picking truth if you're never going to be truthful?"

"You got it." I put the bottle down and answered her question. "After Issa, love ain't in the cards for me. Shit, I don't know if what we had was love cause that shit was one sided as fuck."

"Then, why is it a wrap for you? What if you meet a chick that's willing to match your energy?"

"Then, we can match each other's energy, but a nigga is gonna be heavy in like. Love ain't nothing but a cliché some sad bitch made up."

"Wooooooow," she sang.

"What, you believe in love?"

"I can't even say I believe in love because I've never experienced it. Any dude I messed with there was nothing more than a physical attraction between us." She shrugged.

"Was that your doing or his?"

"What you mean?"

"Was them dudes trying to get to know you and you shot them down just to keep it physical, or was they not interested in anything but the physical?"

"A little of both. Why waste time telling someone your story when they don't really give a fuck anyway?"

"Being vulnerable is having strength."

"I doubt I'll find anyone who makes me so comfortable that my walls come down and I put it all in his hands. Y'all niggas are too trifling for that."

"Truth or dare?"

"Truth."

"You feeling a nigga, huh?" I smirked.

"You know damn well I'm not answering that shit. Pass the bottle."

"Hol' up, what was all that shit you were talking about not answer?"

"Ight, you got it. Am I feeling you? Yeah, you're cool or whatever," she laughed.

"You got a pretty ass laugh," I complimented. "But, that answer not gonna work over here."

"It's the truth."

"Is it tho?"

"Fine but I'ma have to take some shots if I'ma speak the truth."

I passed her the bottle and she threw that shit back like it was Kool-Aid.

"Am I feeling you? I don't know, but I feel something for your ugly ass. Your demeanor and cocky aura is attractive as fuck. The determination you have to get back right is sexy as fuck and that smart ass mouth makes me want to sit this pussy right on it, but that's as far as it goes. The way you talked about ya ex that night and how hurt you were shows me that you're not ready for nothing I have to offer. You put ya faith, trust, and loyalty in the wrong bitch and, because of that, anyone who comes along will have to pay the ultimate price. I know you don't know this, but my heart is too damn bomb to be paying a price off the strength of the last bitch fucking up."

"Damn."

That was some of the realest shit I ever heard and it was straight facts. A price was gon' have to be paid and hoops were gonna have to be jumped through if a bitch wanted to fuck with me, any bitch expect Keisha.

"I'm right huh?"

"Come here."

"Uh, no. You're naked and I know where this can lead to."

"It's only gonna go there if you let it."

"Mhmmm."

"Keisha, bring ya ass over here!" I barked.

"You don't have to yell," she smacked but brought her ass to me. I gripped her hips and lowered her on my lip with my dick resting against her clit.

"Why you have to do the most?"

"I ain't do shit… yet," I laughed.

"Say what you have to say, so I can go about my business please."

Ignoring her, I leaned forward, running my tongue all along her neck and rocking her hips back and forth.

"Wha… what are you doing?" she murmured.

"Showing you that you're the exception," I whispered.

Taking one hand off her hips, I snatched her panties to the side and played in her wetness. Her hips started rocking faster without my help, and I knew what time it was.

"Lift up," I told her.

"For what?"

"Lift up," I repeated.

"We're not doing this Jeezy. Playing is one thing, but I'm not fucking you."

"Lift up."

"Fine but do you have a condom?"

"Nah, and I don't need one. Lift the fuck up 'fore I swallow ya pussy."

"Is that a threat I'm supposed to be scared of?" she giggled.

Feeling like she was taking me for a joke, I flipped her ass back to where her knees were touching her shoulders and her legs rested next to each of her ears. I dove in, kissing her clit roughly and running circles around it. From top to bottom, I licked and slurped her juices up, making her legs shake.

"Stop! Stop! Stop!" she moaned, trying to move my head. Her ass was cumming hard as a muthafucker and I let up. I sucked and spelled random ass words with my tongue until she came for a third time.

"James, I can't... I can't..." she panted.

"What's my name?"

"Huh?"

"You fucking heard me. What's my name?"

"Dadddyyyyyyyy!" she sang, releasing another waterfall in my mouth.

I slurped her clean, then threw the dick at her. She gasped and her stomach tightened when I hit her back wall. I wasn't gonna fuck her too crazy because I needed her to be able to make moves tomorrow. I hit her with the slow stroke and gazed into her eyes. The faces and sexy noises she made had me on edge. I got two more out of her before I was pulling out and bussing on her stomach.

Keisha

I'd never been one to be speechless after sex, let alone to be speechless ever. Talking shit was part of my top five talents, alone with fucking a nigga crazy. I didn't know what the fuck happened with Jeezy, but he had me speechless and questioning my sex game. Usually, I could get a dude to bust quick. It was nothing for me to hit a quick split or to create waves with my ass for a dude to go crazy. None of that applied to last night. Jeezy hit me off with a cute little quickie that had me wanting a full twenty-four hours' worth. In the thirty minutes he had my body, I orgasmed five times and each was more intense than the last. My legs felt like noodles when it was all said and done, but my kitty couldn't stop purring. It was so bad that after, I scurried to my room and stayed there all night.

When I woke up this morning, my ass walked happily into the kitchen and made him breakfast. Jeezy tried joking and talking to me like how he normally did, but my weird ass couldn't find the words to respond. My vibe was all off and this nigga really had me speechless. I ended up eating breakfast in my room because being around him was too much for the moment.

"Aye Kesh, open the door so we can talk," I heard Jeezy say after he knocked.

"Um, I'm busy right now."

"Whatever you got going on can wait. Open this door."

"I'm not dressed Jeezy. Whatever you gotta say can be said through the door."

"Stop playing with me and open the door."

"We can talk later."

"Open this fucking door or I'ma kick the shit in," he threatened.

"Go ahead, this ya shit not min-"

I didn't get a chance to finish my smart comment because this nigga really kicked in the door. It went flying off the hinges and I screamed, being real extra.

"What ya ass screaming for? Ain't that what you wanted, for me to show my ass?"

"No one asked you to show your ass. You chose to kick in your door trying to be Rambo. None of it was necessary and whatever you wanted to say could've waited."

"I'm a stingy nigga. I don't like being on hold."

"I see."

"Why you was acting funny at breakfast?"

"I wasn't acting funny. I cooked and then came in here to eat. What's the problem?"

"Then, why you ain't talk to me? Any other morning your stank breath ass wakes up with mad shit to pop and, now, you have nothing to say."

"Maybe I'm trying to change." I shrugged.

"What's wrong with you?" he asked, not feeding into my lie.

"Nothing."

"Bullshit."

"Why does me not wanting to talk to you have to be bullshit? I wasn't in the mood for conversation."

"That's how you gon' play it?"

"You're making this a bigger deal than what it has to be. Since when did it become a crime to not talk?"

"Sayless Keisha," he gritted

"I know you don't have an attitude."

"I'm good. I'll be back in a few. Keep ya ass in the house."

"Really James?" I questioned, catching an attitude.

He ignored me and walked smooth out of the room and out the front door. I sucked my teeth, then grabbed my phone. If he thought it was going to be that easy, he had another thing coming.

Me: What are you in your feelings for?

Jeezy: Fuck is you texting me for? Didn't I try to talk to ya stupid ass already? Leave me alone, I'm good.

Me: Fuck it if you wanna act funny, then I'ma act funny. Don't be looking for me when you come home.

Jeezy: Kesh, you're really pushing shit. Keep ya stank ass in the fucking house. It's too hot for you to be on some ratchet shit.

Me: You wanna be heard and I wanna be seen.

Jeezy: If I catch ya ass anywhere but in that house, I'ma spankin' you.

Me: Put your hands on me and it'll be murder she wrote.

Jeezy: Ya punk ass is all talk.

Me: Test me if you want.

Jeezy: I said what I said.

Me: Yeah okay. Just be ready to play hide and seek.

Jeezy: You're a cornball. Stop texting me with this dumb shit.

Me: It's only bullshit because I'm matching energy. You got ten minutes to get back to the crib or I'm going out and showing nothing but face and ass.

After that last message, I never got a text back. I gave his ass twenty minutes before I was blowing his phone up. My calls went to voicemail, annoying me further.

"This nigga blocked me," I scoffed.

Flopping on the bed, I laid there pissed off. Jeezy was really doing the most and it wasn't needed. I wasn't talking to him because I knew he was gonna bring up what happened last night and I wasn't in the mood to look stupid in front of him. He did his thing and that gave him bragging rights. I refused to admit just how good the dick was because his ass never going to let it go. On top of that, I was scared of where the conversation would lead to after all the gloating was done.

Just from our little game last night, I knew neither one of us was ready for a relationship, yet we wanted some type of connection with each other. Messing around made the most sense, but we were too stingy and selfish to actually see it through. Who I fucked could only fuck on me and Jeezy just seemed like the crazy jealous type. I mean, the type to see me look in another dude's direction and he'd be on my ass. That shit was toxic on both of our ends because if I caught his ass fucking on the next bitch, it was gonna get ugly. The whole thing would just be too complicated and, if that conversation would've come up, I couldn't see myself saying no to him. Jeezy got on my nerves every second of the day, but I loved being in presence. Truthfully, I wanted more; I just knew I couldn't handle more, and neither could he.

The ringing of my phone caught my attention, giving me a break from my annoying ass thoughts. I snatched it up with the quickness, ready to give Jeezy this tongue lashing.

"You got a lot of fucking nerve putting me on your block list. Nigga, do you not understand the kind of bitch you're fucking with?" I cursed.

"Come on sweetheart, you should know me better than that. What good would it have done to block you when you're the only bitch that's gonna suck my dick on demand," Eddy snarled.

The sound of his voice alone made me cringe, but the disrespect that came out of it had me on the verge of vomiting.

"What do you want?"

"You should know what time it is off the strength of me calling. Meet me at the weed spot. I got a couple of things that need sucking."

"I can't. I'm on my way out to meet a friend."

"Then, bring the bitch along; she got a mouth, don't she?" he laughed. "The last time we were face to face, I explained how things were going to go. You agreed to my terms, so why are you backing out now?"

"I'm not backing out. I just can't meet you at this moment," I explained, trying to find my way out of this situation.

"Man, fuck all of that. When I call, ya ass 'posed to come running. I'm calling, so do ya part and get ya ass over here."

"But-"

"Leave all that but shit where it's at. If opening your eyes every morning means anything to you, your ass will be here in an hour tops!" he barked and hung up.

His words echoed in my head, and I started shaking uncontrollably. The first thing I did without thinking was call Jeezy. He didn't answer but, instead of hanging up, I left a voicemail.

"Jeezy, I really need you to call me. Eddy just called me and... and he wants me to come meet him for a favor. We both know what that means and we know what will happen if I don't show up. I don't know what to do, but I know I can't not go. If you get this message in time, please pull up to the weed spot. He's expecting me in an hour. Don't let me down please, James."

I hung up the phone and, like a zombie, I moved slowly around the room getting ready. I didn't even remember getting in my car and pulling off. All I knew was one minute I was outside of Jeezy's spot and, in the next minute, I was outside of the weed spot. I got out and headed inside, praying Jeezy came through for me before my lips touched a dick.

"I got a bitch named Keisha, she a real dick pleaser," Eddy rapped the moment I walked through the door. I said nothing because nothing nice was about to come outta my mouth.

"What, you don't got a smart comeback today? What was that shit you said last time?"

"I don't remember."

"That's cool cause I do," he chuckled. "You said something along the lines of whatever Keisha I was speaking on ain't this Keisha cause the wonders ya lips work, I'll never experience. There's irony all up and through that bitch huh," he continued to laughed.

"What do you want from me, Eddy?" I smacked.

If I had to suck dick, I was gonna let Eddy know just how low I thought of his ass and how disgusted he made me feel. He wasn't gonna be able to enjoy not a suck when I was done.

"Come on beautiful, stop playing games and get on ya knees. Me and my dudes are in need of some release."

"Dudes? The agreement was never for you and ya nasty ass friends."

"Yeah, well, I'm switching it up. See, I thought this was gonna be a partnership type of agreement. You would get me off and, eventually, you would fall in love with a nigga. I would probably marry ya ass and cheat on you with whatever bitch I felt like it. I would take you through the motions and you'll thank me by letting me spray my seed in ya womb. I had it all figured out and life was gonna be sweet. But, then, I got a call about one of my young boys getting killed. That's when I knew you were playing hardball. What happened Kesh, I thought we had an understanding? You would do as I say and your life would be spared, unlike that nigga of yours. I guess the love you have for ole boy means more than waking up and seeing the sun every morning." He shrugged. "Is that how you feel Kesh? Ya feelings for duke is more important than ya life?"

"I didn't kill anyone and my life means the most," I assured.

"That's not how things are looking. I'm out here looking like a goof in front of my squad because of how you played things. I'm a boss Keisha and, as boss, I can't have my team looking at me crazy. So, what are you going to do to show them that you're team Eddy?"

I looked around the room and there were three other dudes in it. They were all devouring me with their eyes, giving me an uncomfortable feeling. I swallowed hard because as tough as I wanted to be, what could I really do in this situation? I didn't have a gun; my blade wasn't going to take them all out and using it was probably going to put me in a worse position. It felt like all I could do was give in and degrade myself to save my life.

"Man, ain't shit she can do 'cause that nigga of hers is still gonna be left stinking," one of them said.

"Her ass can get laid out right next to him," another chimed in.

"See Keisha, we're at an impasse. My team wants not only Jeezy's head but yours as well. You gotta show them keeping you alive is worth it," Eddy smirked.

The way these niggas all started dropping their shorts felt like this whole thing was rehearsed.

"Can I at least go the bathroom first?"

"Yeah but make it quick."

I nodded, then dashed for the bathroom. I waited a few seconds before running the water in the sink to make it sound like I was peeing. I took my phone out my bag and sent Jeezy a text.

Me: Jeezy, please pull up. I'm putting my faith in you that you'll show up, so please don't let me down. My trust is with you

After that, there was nothing else I could do. I walked out of the bathroom to find these niggas lined up with their dicks in hands. I gulped before walking over to the first dude and dropping to my knees.

James 'Jeezy' Brown

Keisha's ass was fucking hardheaded and I couldn't stand it. When I dipped, I only planned on being gone for thirty minutes or so. I needed to clear my head because for the first time, I didn't understand the type of games that were being played. I never worried about being able to read females because I had Issa. Growing up with her made it easy to read her like a book. Keisha was different and, every time I thought I had her figured out, she was switching shit up. This morning, like any other morning, I thought shit was gonna be cool. We would pop our shit, then end the conversation in laughter. Her ass had a whole different idea because she wasn't giving me nothing.

At first, I thought she was acting awkward because she thought the sex talk was gonna come up. For that reason, I went all the way left and started clowning on her feet. Her shits were wrinkled like a muthafucker but were small like a toddler. The jokes did nothing but make her go in the room and slam the door. That shit had me hot because we were too grown for that shit. When something was on ya mind, you were 'posed to talk about that shit, not run and act like a fucking baby.

Then, being the baby that she was, wanted to text me after I tried to talk to her. Man, once I walked out that door, I ain't give a fuck what was on her mind or what she had to say. It was all null and void. She wanted to test a nigga by talking that I'm going outside bullshit, but she should've known that wasn't gon' work on me. I put her ass on the block list, then went and kicked it with the family.

I needed a calm vibe and my family provided just that. Off the back, my mom asked what chick had me stressing and all I could do was laugh. If anyone knew me like a book, it was my dukes. She saw straight through all the hardness and stayed calling me out on my shit. I told her a female had me stressing, but it wasn't what she thought. Her response was she didn't care what it was like, as long as it wasn't with Issa. Over the years, Issa and my duke's relationship got rocky because of the way she was handling me. I never bothered speaking on it to my mom cause she had her mind made up and I was cool with her decision. Issa wasn't gon' get far in my life anyway.

After kicking it with them for a few, I came back to the crib and it was empty. I took Keisha off the block list and started blowing her phone the fuck up. I shouldn't have had to tell her that going outside right now was a bad look. We left ole boy's body there for Eddy to fine and it wasn't gonna take much for him to trace that shit back to us. I was trying to keep it cool but, the longer she stayed gone and my texts and calls went unanswered, the more nervous I became.

"Fuck this, I'ma just roll up on this nigga," I spat out loud, then called Casper. "Aye, where you at?" I questioned the second he answered.

"At the crib. Wassup, you good?"

"I need you to come roll with me to handle something. Eddy got something that I need back and you know how stubborn that nigga can be."

"Sayless, where you wanna meet up at? You need me to bring Willy or you good with Nelly?" he asked, referring to guns.

"Shit, bring Nelly just in case he tries to play the tough guy. We can meet up at... I'ma call you back," I told Casper and hung up the phone. "Where the fuck you been Kesh?"

"There are 7.5 billion people in the world and, for some reason, people keep picking little ghetto ass Keshia to take advantage of. I shouldn't be too surprised, seeing how my mother was the first person. She's where it all started and, if it's so easy for her to treat me like trash then play the guilt game to get what she wants from me, why do I think anyone else will treat me differently?"

Her tone was dry as fuck and she had this far gone look in her eye. I took her in and nothing seemed to be out of place. Her clothes were straight, hair was in a neat bun, and I couldn't see bruises or signs of struggle. Keshia looked like her regular self, but something was off for sure.

"You good?"

"You want to know why I have a wall up, right? Well, it's my mother's fault. She tears me down every chance she gets and, like a dumb ass, I stand there and take it. I'm 23 and I still allow my mother to belittle me. I guess it's because that's the only type of love I know. I don't even know how I can call that love when she didn't believe that her man was touching me inappropriately. I'm just stupid and, the longer I live and go on in this world, the more signs I get that I'm not supposed to be here."

"Keisha, what the fuck happened?"

"Exactly what was supposed to happen... I'm sorry," she sobbed.

She went in her bag, snatched something out and put her hand to her throat. Shit happened so fast, I didn't know what happened or what she took out her bag until blood was dripping from her neck.

"What the fuck Keshia!" I barked, snatching her up. I held her in my arms and rushed her out to my car.

"Just let me be Jeezy. This is how it's supposed to be," she whispered and had the nerve to smile.

I couldn't say nothing else to her after that cause a nigga was stuck between slapping sense into her dumb ass and whispering that everything was going to be alright. Putting her in the back seat, I snatched my shirt off and tied it around her neck. The cut wasn't deep because the blade wasn't that big. I slammed the door closed and got in the front seat and pulled off. The hospital was where her ass needed to be but, if I did that, they would've put her on a 72-hour hold. I didn't know what was going on, so I couldn't have her locked up in the looney bin. Instead, I took her to a family friend who wouldn't say much, long as I passed her a few bucks.

* * *

"She's going to be fine but, if she tries anything like that again, you need to take her to the hospital. I don't have to explain to you how important it is to get one's mental health in check because you went through you know what with your father."

"I didn't go through shit with that nigga. He did what he did cause he ain't wanna step the fuck up. He left my mother to handle shit and, for that, I'll always spit on that muthafucker's grave!" I gritted.

"Watch your mouth speaking ill of the dead but, more importantly, watch your mouth when speaking about my brother. I know you might not consider this side your family, but my blood pumps through your fucking veins.

Now, your father may not have been able to step up, but I tried to help your mother out; she didn't want anything from us. So, whatever story she is telling you, ask her to tell you the whole truth and not just the parts that make her look good."

"Look, this enough?" I asked, handing her a couple hundreds.

She nodded her head, took the money, and left out the living room. I went over to the couch where Keisha was laid out and kneeled in front of her.

"You wanna tell me what the fuck happened to make you go off the edge?"

"Why couldn't you just let me die?"

"Come on Kesh, you really ain't wanna go out like that."

"Don't tell me what I wanted to do when you don't even fucking know me!" she spat.

"Pipe the fuck down," I warned.

"Fuck you, Jeezy. I haven't asked your bitch ass for one thing but, the moment I do, you wanna come and play fucking God. You don't get to decide who lives and fucking dies."

"I don't but, when it comes to you living or dying, I'ma make that call for you to keep breathing every time," I gritted. "Why we even fucking arguing about this shit? Where was ya ass at?"

"Maybe you should check ya voicemail," she sassed and got up. She pushed my ass, then walked out the apartment. I ran my hand over my face and followed out behind her.

"Fuck a voicemail, I never check that shit. Just tell me where you were at."

"Since I've met you, the one thing you've asked of me is to have trust in you. Today, I was actually willing to put my trust in you but, just like I thought you would, you let me down."

"Yo, stop with the ring around the rosy bullshit and say what needs to be said."

"Eddy called. He wanted me to come through. I tried calling you, but you didn't answer."

"So, you went to see that nigga anyway?"

"What the fuck else was I supposed to do when he was talking about killing me over the fucking phone?"

"Wait for me to get to the fucking crib!" I yelled.

"Don't fucking yell at me for your fuck up! I called you but, because you were in your feelings, you didn't come through."

"What his ass want?"

"What you think," she snickered.

"You did what he asked?"

"I'm not answering that."

"I can't believe this shit," I sighed.

"What is there for you not to believe? You're taking this shit real fucking personal when I was the one sucking on four different fucking dicks!"

"Get the fuck in the car," I growled after she said that shit.

"Fuck you, Jeezy, because this is on you!" she cried.

Hearing her cry fucked me up cause she was right; this was on me. All I wanted was for her to have some trust in me and, when she finally did, I let her down, leaving her in a fucked-up situation.

"I know this is on me, but I'ma make it right," I told her.

"How are you gonna do that? It's not like you can run up on the nigga tonight."

"Just get in the car and let me drop you off. That nigga gon' get handled... tonight."

"How are you gonna do that when my cousins aren't here?"

"I don't really need ya cousins. I got this," I told her cockily.

"Did you not just hear me say I sucked on four dicks? That means Eddy ain't going nowhere by himself. You got a better chance at getting at him if my cousins are-"

"Then, call them the fuck up and tell them get they asses back here! You fucking bitching and crying while I'm trying to make shit right. You either want me to get shit popping or you wanna continue slobbing knobs!"

"Are you dumb?!" she squealed, bringing her and across my face.

I snatched her little ass up real quick, slamming her against the fence that was outside my people's apartment.

"Get the fuck off me, James!"

"Calm the fuck down first and I'll think about it."

"Nigga, I ain't doing shit!"

"Fuck it then!"

I slammed her ass against the gate again and held her there. I was hot as a muthafucker and all the bitching she was doing wasn't helping shit. I ain't give a fuck about dying because when the smoke cleared, that nigga Eddy was going with me. The way he violated Keshia wasn't gon' go unanswered.

"I can't believe you would disrespect me like that, after all I done told your ass," Keshia sobbed.

"Kill all the crying, that shit not gon' help nothing."

"I don't give a fuck! Do you know how fucked up I am right now?"

"That's why I'm trying to go and handle it, but ya ass keep coming up with excuses and shit."

"It's not excuses. I'm trying to make sure you don't die behind what happened to me."

"Dying don't scare me and, if I'm gon' go out, ain't a better way to go than defending your honor. You may not think you're worth the blaze of glory, but you are. So, let me handle this cause I promise I won't let you down."

"We have to stick to the plan. I'll call my cousins and have them come down tomorrow."

"That shit gon' be too late. This gotta get answered tonight Keshia! Look at what you did as a result of the bullshit."

"What I did is a result of holding in issues when I should've let them go. Don't get me wrong. Eddy and them other niggas are gon' get what they got coming to them but, right now, I need you to be here for me."

"I can't do that Keshia," I sighed.

"So, you're really gonna let me down twice in one day."

"Don't do that. I'm trying to right a wrong."

"I know, but making sure I'm good trumps all that."

Gazing into her eyes, I couldn't tell her now. Her words were sincere, but the look in her eyes were begging me to stay with her.

"Ight. But, tomorrow, this shit going down. I'm not dealing with no more disrespect from this nigga, Keshia."

"Neither am I."

I let her go and waited for her to fix her clothes before scooping her into my arms and carrying her to my car. I headed back to the crib thinking about the different ways this nigga Eddy was about to die.

Keisha

"Who would've thought my summer was going to pop off like this?" I laughed awkwardly.

Jeezy and I were sitting in his room on the bed eating and watching TV. I guess you could say the tv was watching us because I doubt either of us was paying it attention. I didn't know about Jeezy, but my mind was stuck and I felt numb all over. The way Eddy treated me was less than humane and had me wanting to wash my mouth out with bleach. I felt like a dog in his presence and felt even lower the longer I went on with the act. It didn't matter how embarrassed I was or how ashamed I might've felt, crying wasn't an option. I did what I was told, then got the fuck on without saying much of anything. Eddy taunted me the whole time and didn't stop until I was pulling away in my car. I kept my emotions in line and told myself I wasn't going to talk about the experience. The best thing for me to do was forget that it happened, the same way I forced myself to forget a lot of the other painful stuff I'd been through. I was completely fine until I walked in here and Jeezy was jumping down my throat.

Seeing and hearing how mad he was with me sent me over the edge. He was blacking on me after just going through one of the worse experiences of my life. That whole rant he went on triggered something and created an emotional overspill. What I told him wasn't meant for his ears. I planned on taking that less than pretty information to my grave. But, once my mouth opened, the words just started coming out and there wasn't a thing I could do. I hated that it was him who heard my darkest secret yet, at the same time, I was relieved.

Carrying around that type of baggage was exhausting and, it didn't matter how deep I buried it or how much I tried to put it out of my mind, a situation like that was always gonna pop up. It was always gonna have to deal with because pain like that was what kept a person humble and guarded. More than anything, I didn't want him looking at me differently because of what I'd dealt with. I didn't need him feeling sorry for me or even trying to fix my situation. What happened was my burden and it was up to me to see the greatness buried deep inside of me; it wasn't meant for him to try and speak greatness into me. I didn't need that and I didn't want that. All I truly wanted was for us to have some type of chance. I was scared out of my mind, but I couldn't keep lying to myself.

"How can you say some shit like that after what you've been through?" he exploded.

"Did I do something because as far as I can see, that tone is way out of context," I spat back.

"Ya ass just came back from doing some degrading shit and you wanna talk about a fucking summer? Only thing we need to be discussing is what time ya cousins touching down."

"Maybe I don't want to think about that right now, especially before I fucking go to bed."

"Real shit Kesh, you don't gotta think about shit. Give me they number and I'll set shit up. You don't gotta do shit but wait to hear from me that it's done. I don't want you 'round that nigga anyway."

"Why are you taking it so personal?" I questioned, moving my food to the side.

I crawled from sitting on the side of him and sat right in front of him. He grabbed me before I could get comfortable and sat me on his lap. I sucked my teeth and tried to move, but he held me in place. His eyes were fixated on mine and I swear my heart skipped more than a few beats.

Without words being said, I knew exactly how he felt about me and I knew it wasn't for play.

"James," I whispered, lowering my hands to where his were placed.

"Don't move my hands!"

"This isn't-"

"This is what needs to happen. Since we've met, you've been questioning me and my actions towards you. I ain't speak too much on it before cause I didn't know what it was. I figured that shit out tho. I'm taking what happened personal because that's exactly what it is to me. You're just not some chick I met in the club and been spending time with because I wanna fuck. You're more than that. I can't put it in words what you are, but you mean something to me. That pain I saw in your eyes, felt in your words, was enough to make me wanna move mountains. I dropped the ball today and that's something I'ma regret for life. Nothing I can do will make up for my downfall, but it can ease ya mind a little. So, when I'm barking on you about putting that call in, it's because I can't stand knowing that nigga is still out there breathing. He don't deserve another 24 hours, let alone 12, but I'ma chill cause I understand you might need some time to ease ya mind. You need to get it off ya chest though and that's what I'm here for. Keeping it locked up ain't gon' do shit but have you putting that funky ass wall back up," he said.

"Who said it was down? What I told you came out by mistake so that doesn't mean I'm an open book. You have to earn the right to truly know me because it's a privilege."

"A privilege it is, but I already earned that shit."

"When?"

"The night I had you screaming my name. What I get you off, five times?" he smirked.

"Nigga bye!" I laughed. "You did ight, but that's not close to being the point."

"Then, put me on and speak from the heart."

"The point is I'm ready to stop bullshitting and lying to myself," I paused to figure out exactly what I wanted to say.

Jeezy had already made it clear what it was hitting for when it came to me. We both knew this wasn't love, but something was here. The vibe was too real and too dope for us to walk away from it. The way he was willing to go to war behind me touched me. I'd heard too many dudes claim to be killers behind a female but, when the time came, the gun action never played out. Jeezy barely knew me and was ready; that was real different.

"Since I've met your annoying ass, I've been coming up with reasons on why we couldn't work. I'm tired and don't wanna do it anymore. I'm scared as hell because I know how Issa played things has you jaded. I'm not saying I'll be any different or that I'll be better; all I'm saying is I'ma be me. What comes with me is a mouth with no filter, a ratchet ass attitude and an attitude that's unmatched. I'm a hot head and hard to handle but, when I ride for someone, I truly ride. My loyalty speaks volumes to those who deserve it, and you deserve it Jeezy. I'ma believer that all things happen for a reason and we came together the way we did for a reason. I don't know what that reason is, but I'm willing to find out. All I ask is that you don't set me up for failure. Don't have me thinking we're in a relationship and all you want is relations. We can keep it simple and just fuck and be friends. Whatever we decide to be, I just need it to be honest and true."

After I was done talking, I put my head down because looking into his eyes was too much.

"What I tell you about ducking the eye contact? When it comes to me, kill all that shy shit. Stand ten behind those words you said because I felt that shit. I'm not good to be in a relationship right now. Too much shit is gonna be happening and the last thing I want is for you to feel like you're taking the backseat."

"That's cool," I sighed.

"Don't give up that easy cause I'm not. A relationship is out the picture, but we can come up with something that fits better. Lay out the terms and I'll follow 'em. I just want you in my life by any means," he explained, caressing my cheek.

I melted into his touch and got lost in his words. I didn't want to be the one to define what we were because he gave that same job to Issa and she fucked it up. Whatever was gonna happen between us needed to be set by him, that way no lines could be blurred and confusion would be out the window.

"I don't wanna lay down the rules. I want you to."

"Word?"

"Yeah. I gotta trust you at some point, right? I'ma trust that you won't have me out here looking goofy behind ya ass."

"You don't gotta worry bout shit, clown makeup ain't never been you no way," he laughed.

I laughed too, then mushed him a little. Our laughter started to fade and our vibe started to take over. Jeezy leaned up to kiss me, but I turned away.

"What's the problem?"

"I can't because I-"

"I don't give a fuck bout none of that shit. You brushed ya teeth, right?"

"Yeah."

"Used mouthwash?"

"Yeah."

"Then, we good. I'm not the type of nigga to punish you behind some shit you did to survive. It's all good. So when I go to kiss my lips, you give me them shits."

"Oh, so my lips are yours now?" I giggled.

"That's what I said, right?" he smirked.

I nodded.

"Ight, give 'em to me then."

I leaned forward, kissing him. His hands roamed my body and my tongue roamed his mouth. The moment was perfect, but what made it better was Jeezy pushing me to the side and telling me that the dick was off limits until business was handle and he could take me on a date. I faked argued with him, calling him pussy. He laughed at me and told me that my pussy was dripping behind that shit he just said. I couldn't do much but roll my eyes and go back to eating my food because he ain't say not one lie. A nigga that could put the pussy on ice just to be a gentleman was a turn on. This was the type of thug shit I liked and what could possibly have me falling in that four letter word.

* * *

"Oh bitch, this is nice, but where the fuck is the furniture?" Bailey announced.

Her and my mom had only been at Jeezy's loft for all of three minutes and already checked out the whole place. I couldn't do much but shake my head because they were one in the same, nosey as fuck.

"Mhmm, I thought I taught your raggedy ass better than this," my mother huffed. "If you were gonna give it away, then the least you could do was give it to a nigga with money. Fucking on a broke nigga ain't gon' do shit but leave your ass broke."

"Dion, will you shut the fuck up? Not everyone wants to think or find love with their pussy," my aunt spat.

"Speak for yaself Diandra. The only way this kitty getting out the box is if a nigga is throwing blue faces," she laughed. "Listen to ya aunt if you want and ya ass is gonna end up with tear stained cheeks and wet pussy."

"So fucking embarrassing," Diandra sassed.

"How, when I'm telling nothing but the truth? Shit, if my logic is embarrassing, what do you call Phour? Her ass done went and got her an elite type of nigga. Her ass is so blinded by the money, she got that boy calling her Alisha," my mother laughed.

"Dion, don't speak on my daughter!"

My aunt got in my mother's face and, being the hood booger that she was, she started taking off her earrings.

"Diandra, stop acting like you don't know my body. I'll beat ya ass all up and down this empty ass piece of shit!"

"Ma!" I yelled.

"No Keisha, let ya mother talk her shit because when I slap the shit out of her, I need her to know it's warranted."

"See a bitch, slap a bitch, hoe!" my mom popped back.

"Alright, that's enough," Kylie announced, standing in between the two. "Y'all are too damn old to be carrying on like this. And, aunty, don't no one know your body. Who the hell taught you that?"

"That's ya momma doing the most. She just mad that Ricky choose me back in the day."

"Ain't no one tripping off that old shit. Ricky only choose you because ya hoe ass was slinging pussy like it was crack," my aunt huffed.

"You're just mad this pussy kept a nigga that broke your heart."

"Okay, I'm done. Ma, you gotta go."

"Call me an Uber and I'll gladly get the fuck on!"

"Done!"

I pulled my phone out and, in a few minutes, her Uber was pulling up and she was out the door. Kylie followed in my footsteps and got one for my aunt too. Once they were both gone, all we could do was shake our heads and laugh. Phour swore up and down that me and her sisters were the ghetto bunch, when we didn't come close to the ghettoness that was our parents. My mother was by far the worse out of the two, but my aunt could get down with the best of 'em.

"Does anyone wanna hear the full story about what happened with Ricky?" Bailey asked out the blue.

"Not even," Kylie said, and I agreed.

"That's the last story I want to hear. Knowing my mother, I'm sure she did some underhanded shit to auntie."

"I'm surprised that mommy let her take her man," Kylie told us. "She's forever preaching about fighting for what we love, yet she let her own sister sleep with the man she was in love with."

"Ugh," I cringed. "Just thinking about the situation makes me sick."

"You ain't never lied," both the twins agreed.

Thankfully, Jeezy had went to meet up with one of his boys, giving me some alone time to fill my cousins in on what I needed them to do. If he would've been here, I would've died behind him seeing my mother's behavior. She was too old to be acting like she was my age. What was more embarrassing was her using today's slang like it was nothing. My mother was too much and, the further I could keep her away from Jeezy, the better. We were just starting to figure things out, and the last thing I wanted was her ass coming and fucking it up or Jeezy fucking her up.

"Alright Kesh, tell us what's going on. You didn't cut our A.C. trip short for nothing," Kylie spoke up.

"I need y'all help."

"We figured that much but our help with what?" Bailey asked.

Taking a deep breath, I ran down what the plan was when it came to Eddy and all that been happening since they left. Of course, Bailey was down with no questions asked. She was into all that thug shit. Kylie, on the other hand, was pissed off and did very little to hide it.

"That's why I don't like that nigga. How the fuck you end up sucking dick, when this nigga was out here begging for your trust and to have faith in him?"

"It's not his fault. We were-"

"Shut the fuck up Kesh cause I don't want to hear it. You're only copping a plea because that nigga laid the dick. down and you got caught up. That nigga is foul and the shit you went through weighs heavy on his fucking shoulders. I can't believe this shit!"

Kylie was going off, and I couldn't do nothing but let her have her moment. If she didn't get her shit off now, then when Jeezy walked through that door, it was gonna be world war III.

James 'Jeezy' Brown

"**R**emember when you said if I needed anything, you'll be down for the cause?" I asked.

I hated coming to my nigga like this because he was done with this life, and I respected that. If I could've went to anyone else, I would've, but I needed my brother on this one.

"Nigga, get to the point cause you know I'm down for whatever."

"Eddy crossed a line and ain't no going back from that shit."

"I thought things were already written in stone for that nigga?"

"They were, but that's when things were strictly on a business level. I was getting at this nigga for not humbling himself and moving his people out of my spot."

"Ight, what changed."

"He disrespected someone close to me and now it's personal."

"I know he ain't violate lil bro?" Casper asked, speaking about my brother.

"Nah, and it wasn't dukes either. He got at ole girl I told you about."

"You tryin' to make shit hot over a bitch?"

Hearing Casper call Keisha a bitch had me blacking. I threw a crisp right to this nigga's jaw and followed up with a left. I ain't bother explain shit to him cause I knew there would be no talking. He was gonna come right back with punches of his own. We ended up tussling for a minute before I held my hands up in surrender. I ain't give in because he was getting the best of me. I did that shit because more pressing matters needed to be dealt with.

"Ight, you got it my nigga," I told him, then spit out some blood.

A nigga's lip was busted, but it was cool cause Casper's nose was leaking just the same.

"Nigga, fuck is going on with you? If I overstepped by speaking ill on shawty, then say that shit. We too grown for the tussling bullshit."

"It's on me and I'll wear it. That bitch word is a trigger. Lil baby is too dope to be disrespected like that."

"Then, say that. I can't respect a female I don't know and I damn sure can't respect a female without knowledge of what she means to you."

"I don't know what she means to me. All I know is I'm not tolerating disrespect of any kind when it comes to her."

"I get it." He nodded, then dapped me up. "What you need me to do?"

Smiling, I told Casper all that I needed from him and he was down for the bullshit. We ended the conversation with him telling me to text him with a time and he'd handle the rest. I told him I got him, then jumped in my car and sped back to the house. With the way I was feeling, Eddy could've got handled within the next five minutes. He had been breathing for too long and, because of it, he was starting to get this cocky nature about 'em. I wasn't feeling that shit, not even a little bit. That nigga wasn't bout shit and only got off on females who couldn't protect themselves.

The nigga already had a death sentence coming but, for that bullshit he did to Keisha, a quick death wasn't gonna happen. Games were about to be played and a lesson was gonna be taught. Any muthafucker that tried coming at me or mine was gonna have to come correct cause if not, I was sparing no lives, families included. By tonight, everything would be a wrap and the summer could get popping like it was supposed to be. I mean, a summer in Brooklyn wasn't shit without a few shootouts and bodies dropping. That shit was eerie, but it was the life you became accustomed to when you lived in the hood. I ain't know if it was gonna be the life I lived forever; it was just how I was giving it up now. The rest of the summer wasn't gon' be hectic like it was now. I planned on slowing shit up for Keisha's sake. I couldn't be trying to figure out shit with her and doing shit that could take me away from her. A nigga had to take back the crown and make sure he still had his bitch by his side.

An hour later, I was walking into my crib and straight into an open palm.

"Nigga, you got a lot of fucking nerve. How the fuck you gonna have my cousin ask if we can set up a nigga you got problems with?"

I didn't comprehend shit shawty was saying because a nigga was trying his hardest not to slap her silly ass back. Hands being put on me wasn't something I tolerated. I already had to tell Keisha bout her fucking hands and she should've relayed that message to her cousin. Growing up, my dukes didn't put hands on me and, for that reason alone, neither was any other bitch.

"Kylie, what the hell are you doing?" Keisha questioned, shocked. "I already explained the whole situation to you. This isn't anymore Jeezy's faults than it is mine."

"Keep telling yourself that if you want to stupid. As a man, when you told this dumb ass Eddy had it in his mind that y'all was working together, he should've went to him and set the record straight."

"Kylie, sit your ass down and stop all the dramatics. You lucky his ass didn't swing back. You can't just be swinging on folks."

"You would know huh," she snickered at her sister.

"Bitch, don't run my business cause I'll do what this nigga didn't and park your ass. Go find someone to play with Kylie because you know this ain't even close to what you want."

"Kesh, let me holla at you for a second."

"Whatever you need to say to her, you can say in front of me. Nothing us a secret in this bitch anymore."

"I'm trying to keep shit pg, handle ya blood," I told Keisha.

"Kylie, you're overstepping right now. I asked a favor of you. If it was going to be a problem, all you had to do was say no."

"I don't have a problem helping you and you know that. What I have a problem with is this nigga strolling up in this bitch like he owns the place."

Chuckling, I replied, "It's my name that's on the deed for this loft, so a nigga do own this bitch. And if you put ya hands on me again, you're gonna find yaself playing in traffic."

"Is that a threat?" She smacked, walking towards me.

"Nah, that shit is some important info that ya ass needs to know."

"Nigga, I don't need to know shit. What you need to know is that-"

"Aye Kesh, when the last time ya cousin got piped down? Her attitude nasty as fuck and I know someone who can fix that."

"I wouldn't dare lay next to any nigga that's in your circle. Fucking trash ass niggas."

"Ya blood love this trash ass nigga," I laughed.

"James," Keisha said, giving me the eye.

"Give ya girl that eye. I came in this bitch peaceful as fuck, just to get slapped about some bullshit."

"Ain't nothing bullshit about wanting to hear an apology."

"You don't gotta hear shit cause I did nothing to you. Kesh heard what I needed to say, and she's good. Stop sticking ya nose into situations that don't concern you. I get the overprotective role, but it's not necessary. I dropped the ball once, best believe that shit ain't gon' happen again."

"It better the fuck not because I play with them thangs and them thangs don't miss," Kylie smirked.

"Oh, shut ya ass up. You only know how to shoot a gun because of me. Jeezy, if you need a bitch on ya team, holla at me. I'm straight on all levels."

"Ya fam is wild," I chuckled, letting the shit prior go.

Keisha was standing off to the side and I wasn't feeling that shit. I caught her eye and patted my lap, letting her know that's where she needed to be. Her ass did like I wanted and sat on my lap.

"Come on with the hugged up shit," Kylie sassed.

"I think you were right Jeezy. She need some dick."

We all busted out laughing, with Kylie swearing up and down her sex life was straight. To keep the good vibes going, I ordered food and rolled up a few blunts. Shit was going down tonight but, for the meantime, I wanted shit to be chill. Couldn't have any of 'em on edge cause that's how mistakes happened. A calm and clear mind was the key to getting this shit accomplished.

* * *

"You sure they can pull this shit off?" I asked Keisha.

We were parked a few cars down from the pool hall Eddy was at. Kylie and Bailey had been in there for a little more than an hour and hadn't said shit. I wasn't expecting them to call, but I told they ass to text Keisha when contact was made.

"Stop worrying, they got it. Kylie might be an overprotective parent but, when it's time to turn up, she can handle herself," she assured.

"I'm just saying, she shoulda hit ya line by now."

"She probably couldn't get to her phone." She shrugged, then went back to gazing out of the window.

"You ight?"

"I'm good."

Her eyes darted right back out the window and I knew she was on some bullshit. This was the reason I didn't want her ass coming. Originally, she was gonna wait for me at the crib but, last minute, she was talking about she wanted to come. We damn near tore each other's heads off over the situation. If it wasn't for her cousins getting in the middle and saying they weren't doing shit unless Keisha rode, she would be in the crib crying. Keisha wasn't ready for this shit, but she was gonna have to learn that the hard way.

"I told you they could handle it," she said.

Looking out the window, I caught a glimpse of Kylie, Bailey, and Eddy getting into his car. I smirked cause now it was game time.

Keisha

My hands were sweating like crazy when we pulled up to the abandoned warehouse. I got out and my legs felt like they were going to collapse. My heart was in my chest and my breathing was slower than normal. I was on edge because this was the moment of truth. Jeezy thought he was gonna be the one to handle Eddy and the rest of those dudes, but it was me who was going to end them all. I couldn't let Jeezy get this one because it was too personal. I degraded myself in order to survive and, now, I wanted to see each of them niggas do the same.

"You ready?" Jeezy asked, grabbing my hand.

"As I'll ever be." I half smiled and held his hand a little tighter as we walked inside.

It was dimly lit in here, but I could see so I wasn't tripping. We went through a few doors before we got to our destination. On the walk in, I was greeted by six sets of eyes and three bodies tied up.

"How did you-" I started to ask Jeezy, but he cut me off.

"I told you everything was gonna be handled. You don't have to worry about any of them niggas after tonight."

Smiling at him, I leaned up and kissed him deeply. For the first time in my life, I felt truly protected.

"Ight, we got time to handle that later."

I wiped his mouth, then walked further into the room with him by my side.

"Wassup up niggas?" he asked in a sinister tone.

Jeezy went over to each dude and ripped the tape off their mouths.

"I said wassup niggas! When a boss is talking, you fucking reply!" he demanded.

They all mumbled different greetings and the sounds of their voice sent chills up my spine. As if I was going through the situation for a second time, I could feel their hands on the back of my head, forcing their dick deeper down my throat than it already was. Out of nowhere, I started gagging and shaking uncontrollably.

"You ight Keisha? What's wrong?" Jeezy quizzed. I couldn't do nothing but hold my chest and wheeze.

"She probably still got my dick down her throat!" one of the niggas laughed.

Jeezy stepped away from me and, just like that, I was fine. My breathing was normal, but my heart was beating double time. Rage filled up inside of me and, without thinking, I snatched a gun off a table I didn't realize was there and shot one of the niggas. The gun shot caught everyone's attention and the dude that Jeezy was beating on started singing a different tune.

"Aye Jeezy, you know we didn't wanna do ya girl like that. Eddy was coming at us sideways and talking that murder shit if we didn't participate."

"Eddy must've been the reason you said that slick shit a minute ago too, huh?"

"Untie him Jeezy!" I demanded.

"That ain't how this is gonna be played."

"I said untie him."

Jeezy tried saying something else but shit up quick when I killed the second nigga.

"Untie him because this is gonna go how I want it to go."

"You got it lil baby," he told me, then untied the smart mouth.

"Go pull down their jeans."

"Man, I ain't about to-"

"Jeezy."

Just like that, ole boy was knocked to the floor and being stomped out. I cleared my throat, and Jeezy stopped.

"I said pull their jeans the fuck down!"

This time, he did what I asked.

"Their boxers too and pull their dicks out."

"You gotta be fucking kidding me. I'm not pulling out no one's dick."

I left off one shot and growled, "Does it look like I'm fucking kidding? You didn't have a problem seeing dicks when you were degrading me. You damn sure didn't have a problem watching me suck the next man's dick. You stood right there and jacked off until it was your turn, so don't bitch up now. Do as I say or be one ball short."

"You fucking bugging. Jeezy, get ya girl."

Shaking my head, I stormed over to where dude was and kicked him in the face. He fell to the ground, and I bent over to snatch his stuff down. Just like the bitch he was, he started peeing the second I pressed the gun to his dick.

"See, I was gonna make you suck both of those dead dicks and record for ya family to see. But, after much consideration, I'ma do you one better." I stroked the trigger, letting one go in his ball sack. It exploded and blood gushed everywhere. His ass was still alive and I was glad.

"Ahhh fuck!" he cried.

Tears were streaming from his eyes but that meant nothing to me. I sat on his chest and pressed the barrel of the gun to his forehead.

"It's niggas like you that give street dudes a bad name. It's pussy ass niggas like you that make it hard for bitches like me but, see, I done did women a favor. We won't have to worry about ya rat ass reproducing any pussy ass niggas."

"Handle ya business cause we got that other thing," Jeezy said.

"Be lucky I have to go because torture is something I find myself taking an interest in."

Before getting up, I slammed the gun in his face repeatedly. It wasn't enough to just kill him; I wanted him to feel the pain I've been dealing with. By the time I was done, the nigga was a centimeter away from death. Putting a bullet in him and ending it would've been too easy. His ass deserved to die slow, so I allowed him to do just that. I moved away from him and tossed Jeezy the gun.

"Don't kill him, let him bask in his pain until he takes his last breath."

Jeezy said nothing but grabbed up the other guns that were still on the table. We walked out of the warehouse and jumped in the car, headed to our next destination.

* * *

"Aye, let me holla at you before we go up there," Jeezy said, stopping me from getting out the car. "You wanna talk about what you did back there?"

"Nope. All I want is to get this whole thing over and done with."

"I've watched the toughest nigga crumble after catching his first body. I just want to make sure that you're good."

"If he crumbled, then he couldn't be the toughest. When I said I'm good, I mean it."

"You sure you ain't tryna tell me what you think I wanna hear?"

"Come on Jeezy, do I look like that type of chick? I don't speak anything less than real. I'm good, trust me."

"Ight."

"After tonight, I won't have to worry and we catch a smooth summer vibe. For right now, I need you to stop worrying."

"You got it lil baby." He smiled.

I got out of the car and checked my phone to send Kylie a text, letting her know I was on my way up. When we got to the entrance of the building, I turned towards Jeezy and put my hand on his chest.

"I need you to let me handle this by myself."

"Get the fuck outta here Keisha. That nigga needs to see me behind that shit he did to you."

"No, the only person he needs to see is me. I can't have you fighting my battles."

"It's not about what you can't have. It's about me being a man and handling man shit. What you did back at the warehouse was cute, but none of that is going down here. This kill is mine," he gritted lowly.

"I appreciate you wanting to protect me and trust me when I say I feel protected, but this is something I have to do. We can't start off whatever this is with you coming to my rescue. If we want *us* to work, then we both have to carry the weight and fight our own demons. Eddy was yours to handle when all of this popped off; right now, he's mine and you have to let me do this."

I was gripping his shirt, pleading for him to understand where I was coming. It was all about growth and getting back at this nigga was gonna be ultimate growth for me. I'd let so many people come into my life just to hurt me and never once did I do anything. This was where it was going to end. I was over the bullshit and ready to get with all the antics. Muthafuckers were gonna learn to not play with me cause I wasn't the friendly type.

"Kesh, this ain't what I wanted for you," he started, and I jumped right in.

"It's not what you wanted, but it's what needs to happen."

"Let me finish!" he barked. "This isn't what I wanted because you deserve better than this type of lifestyle. Carrying and killing muthafuckers ain't for you, and we both know it. That's why I was ready to bear it for you. I wasn't out here rushing to get back at Eddy for my own selfish reasons. An energy I had towards this shit was off the strength of you. I don't know how you did it, but you got a nigga reconsidering some shit. Regardless of what comes out of this shit, it's gonna me and you for a lifetime. I'ma always hold shit down and be ready for war behind you. It's nothing when it comes to you and that's on everything."

If I wasn't trying to hold back my emotions, I probably would've cried after hearing what Jeezy said. In his own way, he let it be known that I meant as much to him as his mother and brother did. That was deep because he held them at the highest of highs. Nothing I said could've matched his words. All I could do was kiss him after that and hoped that he got the memo about the feelings being mutual.

"Man, take ya emotional ass in there and handle business. You got five minutes. If you're not walking out these doors, I'm coming up and wrapping shit the fuck up, ight?"

"I got you, but give me ten minutes."

"Hurry ya ass up."

He grabbed me, pulled me into a hug and tucked a gun in the small of my back. I walked inside and stepped on the elevator, feeling more confident than ever. When I got to the apartment door, I knocked on the door and walked in once Bailey opened it. Eddy was tied up on the bed spread eagle, looking like the bitch that he was. I could hear mumbles coming from both of my cousins, but I couldn't comprehend what they were saying. All I saw was Eddy and flashbacks of what I had to endure.

Moving close to the bed, I pulled the gun out and said, "Do you have any last words?"

"Fuck is this supposed to be a nigga's death?" Eddy laughed. "I should've known that nigga Jeezy wasn't gonna handle shit himself. That nigga always been pussy. Keisha, you really let this nigga play you out like that after he left you to suck on four dicks."

His words taunted me and his voice made the hairs on the back of neck stand up. Even though I was pointing the gun at him, his ass was still running his mouth. He was looking straight at his killer and had the nerve to take me as a joke. I was tired, too fucking tired, and my mother was to blame. It all started with her making me feel like I was less than. It then trickled to her boyfriend, who couldn't keep his hands to himself, and somehow made its way to Eddy and his baboons. The trauma and embarrassment seemed like a never-ending ripple effect. If this was the old me, I probably would've accepted it for what it was and just buried the pain. Thankfully, I wasn't the old me and, thankfully, I had someone like Jeezy in my corner. The savage had been woken up, so now it was time to play.

"Bring his ass into the bathroom," I told my cousins, snapping out of my daze.

"How the fuck are we gonna get his big ass in the tub? It took both of us getting naked just to get him in the bed and tied up," Bailey complained.

"She ain't lying. I had to kiss her crusty lip ass," Kylie chimed in.

"Shut the fuck up because my lips are smooth as fuck," Bailey snapped.

"This shit gotta be a fucking prank," Eddy chuckled.

Letting a shot off, I grilled all three of them before saying, "I don't give a fuck what had to be done. All I care about is what's about to get down. Like I said, bring his ass into the bathroom and drop him in the tub!"

Both girls sucked their teeth so, to make their job easier, I shot Eddy twice: once in each kneecap.

"Gag his stupid ass!" I growled after he screamed out like a bitch.

Both Bailey and Kylie were looking at me like I was someone else. I refused to explain my actions, so I went into the living room to find something that would get the job done. Luckily, the apartment belonged to a crackhead because these muthafuckers always had useless shit in their crib. I found an old ass iron and brought it into the bathroom, just as they were pushing Eddy into the tub.

"Run the water," I ordered.

The water started flowing, then the tub started to fill up. Eddy began begging for his life, but his words fell on deaf ears. I pulled the iron in and waited for it to get hot. Once again, my cousins were talking, but I couldn't make out a single word they said. I was so dazed out that I didn't realize the iron had found its way into the bath water until Eddy's voice was no longer amongst the mix.

"Keisha, you ight?" Bailey questioned, shaking me.

"It's over Keisha. Snap out of it!" Kylie snapped.

"I'm fine, get the fuck off me," I sassed.

"Uh huh bitch, don't catch and attitude like we just didn't do some borderline nasty shit for your ass," Bailey smacked.

"Shut up and get out of here," I told them.

"We can walk out of here together," Kylie offered.

"Nah, y'all go ahead and tell Jeezy that I'm fine."

"Kesh, we're not about to leave you alone."

"I said I'm good, just go please."

"Come on Kylie because I'm feeling unappreciated like a muthafucker."

I rolled my eyes at Bailey because her dramatics weren't necessary. They left out the apartment and I just stood there gazing at Eddy's lifeless body. I thought killing him was going to give me a sense of satisfaction, but it did nothing for me. I still felt empty and I felt even worse about myself. Tears started to flow and soft cries left my mouth. I was so confused by my actions and the way I was feeling that I didn't wait for Jeezy to come up to the apartment. I cleaned off whatever blood I had on my clothes, then snuck out the back of the building. I jumped in a two-dollar cab and had it drop me off at the train station.

Epilogue

James 'Jeezy' Brown

"**S**he's ready to see you," Kylie said, coming out to my car.

"Just let me know if she's good or not."

"You can go see yourself."

"Fuck that. I have no words for her," I gritted.

Keisha really had me in my feelings behind the stunt her ass pulled. I thought letting her take care of Eddy was the right move. I figured it would allow her to get some of that pent up anger off her chest and it'd be easier for her to move on. That shit backfired like a muthafucker. When her people came out the building and told me what went down, I rushed up to the apartment and her ass was gone. I couldn't run after her cause we had four bodies that needed disposing. I had my brother meet me at the crack head house and I had Casper go back to the warehouse. We got rid of any and everything that could lead back to us; then, I dipped.

The first place I went was my crib. She wasn't there, so the next place I hit was her mom's house. I started to run up in that bitch until I remembered the bullshit her mom's had put her through. I had nothing but ill intentions for that lady so, to spare Keisha any more pain or drama, I stayed parked outside and had Kylie go and check on her. Kylie told me she was straight, but she didn't want to see anyone. I was hot as fuck but respected her decision. I stayed parked outside her mom's for the last seven days, waiting for her to walk out the building. The only time I left was to wash my ass at Kylie's spot. All I wanted was for her to come out, so we could speak about shit. Her ass never came but had the nerve to have Kylie come get me. That was some straight bullshit and I wasn't here for it.

"At what point are you going to realize that this isn't about what you have to say to her? She needs to talk to ya big headed ass, so a conversation is what the two of you are going to have."

"I'm good. I got business to handle."

"Bullshit. You haven't been handling business and we both know the time to get at all them niggas and establish leadership was right after Eddy was handled. You put that shit on the back burner for my cousin, so it being on chill for a few more minutes won't hurt."

"Whatever. Tell her bring her ass down here."

"Okay, and be nice or I'ma have to beat ya ass."

Chuckling, I replied, "Even ya ass don't believe that shit."

"Try me nigga," she joked and headed for the building.

Kylie thought I put shit on hold, but that wasn't close to the truth. I might've been waiting on Keisha, but I knew the money wasn't going to wait on me. I had Casper letting all them niggas know that I was back on my bully. Whoever didn't like it was free to leave but, when I made my presence known, they were gonna drop like flies. A few wasn't fucking with it and, when I was done here, I was shooting to where they was at and shutting shit down. I didn't have time for games with these niggas because the next move was to take over 25th street. I had been in talks with Worm about all of Coney Island being mine. It was only gonna be a matter of time but, for the time being, I needed to handle the matter at hand.

"Are you gonna unlock the door?" Keisha spat, trying to yank the passenger door open.

"Nah, you can say whatever you need to say right there."

"Don't act like that Jeezy."

"How else am I supposed to act? You begged me to let you do something that I knew was gonna break you. Then, you had me sitting out here waiting for your ass for seven days straight. That's some bullshit and you know it."

"I didn't have you waiting out here, you chose to."

"Guess I can say I made the wrong choice."

"Let me in James because shutting me out isn't going to fix nothing."

I hit the lock and she jumped in and grabbed me by the face, trying to kiss me.

"Chill with all that shit and say what you need to say," I told her, mushing her.

"You're really tripping on me because I needed time to wrap my head around all that happened?"

"I ain't tripping behind you needing time. I got a fucking problem with you acting like you couldn't pick up the phone and explain that shit to me. You think I don't know what you did isn't easy? I understand that shit better than anyone. All you had to do was keep it a buck with me and not shut me out. I thought we were building a foundation for us to create a house on? The way you went about things ain't how that shit work. I've been shut out by a bitch once. I'm not fucking with that shit again, especially with ya ass."

"I'm sorry. I didn't realize you would take it so personally."

"How the fuck else was I supposed to take it?" I gritted.

"I don't know!" she shouted. "All I know is that I needed time to figure some things out and get back right. I've come to terms with a lot and I'm ready."

"Ready for what?" I asked, not really giving a fuck.

"I'm ready for us. I thought I couldn't jump into something with you because I didn't know you, but that's bullshit. I don't need to know you on a personal level to know that wherever you are is where I want to be. I know you on a spiritual level because our souls are connected. We have soul ties and not on that toxic shit either. I'm as connected to you as you are to me." She smiled.

"Take a ride with me right quick."

"I'm already in the car with you so pull off."

I gazed into her eyes for a second to see if all that shit she was talking was true. Nothing about her said she was lying, so I nodded my head and pulled off. The ride was silent, but I could see Keisha was on edge. She had just put herself on the line and I ain't say shit. We drove around for a good hour and a half before I pulled up alongside a white Honda Accord Coupe.

"Whose car is that?" she asked.

"Yours."

"Where did you get money to buy me a fucking car?" she asked with her mouth hanging open.

"You think I hit up Eddy without cleaning him out? Fuck outta here," I chuckled. "This ya shit lil baby. The rest of his cash is in the trunk. I know it doesn't make up for what that nigga did to you but shit it's-"

"Thank you!" she screamed, then kissed me.

I kissed her ass back and letting go didn't feel like an option. Her hands went under my shirt and mine undid her shorts. Saying fuck the world, I sat Keisha on my dick and told her to ride my shit.

"I love you, Jeezy," she whispered in my ear.

I already knew what it meant to say that shit back to her, but I couldn't see myself not saying it. Keisha came into my world and turned shit upside down for the better. I wasn't sure what the fuck was gonna come of us, but I knew I was gonna keep her close.

"I love ya crazy ass too."

The End!!

Also Check Out :

Phour A.M. In Brooklyn